"It would be so much easier," Hannah said, "If you threw me over your shoulder and carried me into the cabin."

"Believe me, I've thought about it a time or two," Ryder said. "The only thing stopping me is that I need to know you'll be as crazy as I expect to be when we finally make love."

Hannah suddenly found it impossible to breathe. She knew her heart was still beating. Her blood was pulsing through her veins like molten lava. It was her lungs that seemed to have stopped functioning. And her mind didn't have a single coherent thought. But she could feel . . .

Ryder heard the hitch in her breathing and saw the stunned desire in her green eyes. He could have resisted if she'd said no.

His callused hands framed her face as he crushed her mouth beneath his, and her taste exploded on his tongue like fine brandy. "If you want me to stop, you'll have to tell me now, Hannah. A few more seconds of touching you, kissing you, and I won't be able—"

"If you stop now, I'm afraid my heart will quit beating. . . ."

WHAT ARE *LOVESWEPT* ROMANCES?

They are stories of true romance and touching emotion. We believe those two very important ingredients are constants in our highly sensual and very believable stories in the LOVESWEPT line. Our goal is to give you, the reader, stories of consistently high quality that may sometimes make you laugh, sometimes make you cry, but are always fresh and creative and contain many delightful surprises within their pages.

Most romance fans read an enormous number of books. Those they truly love, they keep. Others may be traded with friends and soon forgotten. We hope that each LOVESWEPT romance will be a treasure—a "keeper." We will always try to publish

LOVE STORIES YOU'LL NEVER FORGET BY AUTHORS YOU'LL ALWAYS REMEMBER

The Editors

Loveswept® 650

TAME A WILDCAT

PATT BUCHEISTER

BANTAM BOOKS
NEW YORK · TORONTO · LONDON · SYDNEY · AUCKLAND

TAME A WILDCAT

A Bantam Book / November 1993

LOVESWEPT® *and the wave design are registered*
trademarks of Bantam Books, a division of
Bantam Doubleday Dell Publishing Group, Inc.
Registered in U.S. Patent
and Trademark Office and elsewhere.

If you would be interested in receiving protective vinyl covers for your
Loveswept books, please write to this address for information:

Loveswept
Bantam Books
P.O. Box 985
Hicksville, NY 11802

ISBN 0-553-44331-3

Published simultaneously in the United States and Canada

Bantam Books are published by Bantam Books, a division of Bantam Dou-
bleday Dell Publishing Group, Inc. Its trademark, consisting of the words
"Bantam Books" and the portrayal of a rooster, is Registered in U.S. Patent
and Trademark Office and in other countries. Marca Registrada. Bantam
Books, 1540 Broadway, New York, New York 10036.

PRINTED IN THE UNITED STATES OF AMERICA

OPM   0 9 8 7 6 5 4 3 2 1

I would like to thank Susan Eisner for her valuable help in researching the Navajo Native American culture. I hope I have conveyed respect and admiration for the Beautiful Rainbow of the Navajo.

TAME A
WILDCAT

PROLOGUE

When he thought of how well his matchmaking plans for his four adult children were working out, King Knight felt downright smug. He was about to accomplish the finest masterpiece of his life.

Grandchildren.

Entering the rose garden, King made a mental note to tell Cyril Beech, the head gardener, to trim back the boxwood hedge to make the entrance wider. His four children would no longer be entering the flower garden in single file when they came home.

King smiled to himself, enjoying the immense satisfaction of having his carefully wrought plans working out so well. Even the sight of the estate's crusty old gardener couldn't ruin King's good mood that day. Although the pungent odor from the fertilizer Cyril was generously spreading around the bases of King's late wife's rosebushes was making King's eyes water, he didn't turn around and walk away.

As King approached, Cyril lifted his grizzled head, his usual flat cap perched precariously on top. An aged tweed coat worn over a wool plaid shirt, complete with knotted knit tie, hung loosely on Cyril's spare frame. Brown wool trousers a size too big were belted tightly at the waist, giving the elderly man the look of a rumpled hourglass. Not for the first time, King wondered just how old Cyril was. As long as King had known the man, who'd been his in-laws' gardener and now worked for him, Cyril had appeared to be ancient.

Cyril gave King one of his wide-eyed stares, which, given his heavy brows, always reminded King of a nearsighted owl. "Good morning, guv," he muttered, nodding and touching the bill of his cap with a grimy finger.

"Yes, it is, Cyril," King agreed. "Even though a spot of sunshine would be welcomed," he added, looking up at the dreary sky. The sun was the one thing he missed the most, other than not having his wife by his side. "Is that fragrant stuff the fertilizer you asked me to order from the mushroom farm?"

With almost a loving touch, Cyril lifted a small amount in his ungloved hand. "'Tis the best there is, sir. Ya can't get no better than horse manure that's been cleaned by mushrooms planted in it. That's a fact."

"I'll take your word for it," King murmured warily, taking several steps back in case Cyril invited him to closely examine the object of his obvious affection. Quickly changing the subject, he said, "Since Knight's Keep is going to be resembling Noah's Ark from now on, I'd like you to arrange for one of the lads to assist you in enlarging the entrance to the flower garden."

Cyril scrubbed callused fingers across the gray stubble covering the lower part of his face as he considered King's statement. The fact that his hand had only seconds ago been handling horse manure apparently didn't faze the elderly man one bit.

"Noah's Ark, sir?"

"You might have noticed we have been blessed with female company of late. The boys now travel in pairs like the animals in Noah's Ark."

"Two of 'em, anyways," mumbled the gardener. "Mr. Michael complained that none of the roses are in bloom. He wanted to pick some for

Miss Harrold. I told him she could come see them when they bloom in the spring."

"It is unfortunate that the roses aren't at their best now, Cyril. The time of year was one thing I didn't consider in my plans. I can't think of a more romantic gesture than presenting a rose to a beautiful lady."

"That's 'cause there ain't none better." Cyril's tone became slightly exasperated. "Is all four of 'em gettin' married? If ya want roses from the Keep for their weddings, I hafta warn ya, it'll be a while before they start budding."

"So far, Michael and Turner are the only ones to have definite plans to wed, and no dates have been set as yet. I'm expecting Ryder next. Silver might take a little longer. I will inform them all of the availability of the roses in spring, however, in case they wish to include Knight's Keep roses in their wedding plans."

Cyril made a disgruntled sound. "I suppose it can't be helped. That romance stuff hits even the best homes."

"That it does," King agreed with a laugh.

He resisted telling Cyril there could soon be children again at Knight's Keep. The poor man was depressed enough with just the thought of the upcoming weddings depleting his supply of roses. Knowing children would be tramping on the grass and picking his flowers would undoubtedly cause the gardener even greater distress.

King himself could hardly wait to hear the happy laughter of his grandchildren. The thought of Knight blood coursing through another generation eased the occasional stabs of his conscience. He wasn't interfering in his children's lives, he rationalized. He was just giving fate a badly needed nudge.

As with Ryder's situation. If left to his own timetable, King's third son would stay single for years, searching for the next adventure, taking a chance on finding another bonanza strike.

Ryder might not realize it yet, but Dawn Skylark's granddaughter would be his greatest challenge.

ONE

The fine citizens of Bacon Ridge made Ryder Knight feel as welcome as a skunk at a picnic.

Luckily, he hadn't had to ask anyone how to find the Trading Post. From the glares he'd been receiving, he'd probably be directed to the next town. He didn't know what the residents' problems were, but he was becoming irritated by all the cold stares and sideways glances he was getting as he walked from the parking lot to the entrance of the Trading Post.

But then, he thought grimly, it didn't take much to annoy him lately. Not knowing why he'd been so edgy and restless the last couple of months hadn't improved his lousy disposition. Fed up with his irritable attitude, he'd come up with the theory that he was spending too much time behind a desk and not enough out in the field.

Which was why he was sweating under the hot midday sun in the middle of the week walking through a dinky one-horse town, instead of sitting comfortably in his spacious air-conditioned office in Houston.

Stopping in front of the Trading Post, he scanned the building. A large sign made of cut-out wooden block letters was perched on top of the narrow shingled roof, which extended out over a wooden sidewalk. The letters spelled out TRADING POST. The storefront had been designed to resemble the style of general stores from the days of stagecoaches and covered wagons. To add a further Old West touch, two hitching posts flanked the three wooden steps that led up to a covered porch, which sprawled from one side of the store to the other. Located on the far edge of the main street, the store had more parking space than any other business in Bacon Ridge— probably, Ryder guessed, because it did the most business.

He gave the window displays of Native American pottery, Navajo jewelry, and the typical advertising signs a brief glance before he pushed open the door. Over his head, a cowbell loudly announced his arrival. A plump woman behind the counter continued pouring dried beans into a paper sack sitting on a large scale without once looking his way.

Ryder didn't need to ask if she was the woman he had come to see. He could tell she wasn't. The only similarity between this woman and the picture of Hannah Corbett he'd seen was that both women had black hair. The woman behind the counter, though, was pushing fifty easily, and he knew Hannah Corbett had recently celebrated her thirtieth birthday. From what he could tell by the photo he'd found in the file someone had put on his desk, the woman he was seeking was also much taller than the clerk and about forty pounds lighter.

And she had stirred his loins in a way no other woman had managed to do in a very long time. That response alone had piqued his interest. It had also reminded him of how long it had been since he'd been with a woman. When he'd had difficulty remembering the occasion and the woman's face, he had concluded that he'd found another reason for his irritable mood. When a one-dimensional photograph could turn him on as if he were a teenager with his first girlie magazine, he knew he needed a change of scenery, a cold shower, or a shrink. He'd settled for the trip from Houston to Bacon Ridge, Arizona.

Now all he had to do was find out how he could find Hannah Corbett.

He studied the clerk as he thought about his approach. The woman looked as friendly as a grizzly bear with a sore paw.

She was dressed in a black velvet blouse and deep red full skirt, her hair bundled up and clubbed at the back of her head in the traditional Navajo style. As she waited on the customers, she spoke a language Ryder couldn't understand but had heard spoken as he'd walked the one-block commercial area of Bacon Ridge.

He watched with growing respect as the clerk lifted a twenty-five-pound sack of flour without showing any sign of strain. She was obviously someone he wouldn't want to tick off. As he waited for her to finish with the other customers, he admired the numerous silver bracelets around her wrists and the squash-blossom necklace, heavy with turquoise, that lay against the luscious black velvet of her top.

After the last customer had completed her purchase, he stepped forward. He didn't let the instant guarded expression on the clerk's face stop him from asking, "I'm looking for Hannah Corbett. I was told she owns this store. Could you tell me where I could find her?"

The Navajo woman shook her head. "She not here."

He'd already figured that out for himself.

He was about to phrase his question differently when the sound of something heavy being dropped in the back of the store made the clerk jump nervously. A woman's voice floated out to them, cursing fluently and imaginatively in Spanish, and he smiled at the ripe choice of cusswords being directed at some object. His knowledge of Spanish was extensive, especially the raw language tossed around on a drill site, and he was impressed with the woman's colorful vocabulary.

Glancing at the clerk, he caught her look of apprehension as she stared at him. Then she turned her head to look at a curtain-covered doorway at the rear of the store as though she were expecting some dreaded object to appear.

Ryder didn't need to ask what her problem was. Her expression told him everything he needed to know. And she knew it.

"Miss Hannah is very busy," she stated bluntly when he started to walk in the direction of the back room. "Come back later."

Ryder was more curious than ever to meet Hannah Corbett. Any woman who could cuss with such versatility was bound to be interesting.

"It's all right," he assured the clerk over his shoulder. "I won't take up much of her time."

He could feel the clerk's dark gaze boring into his back as he stepped around the display shelves that stood between him and his objective. He half expected the woman to run over and stand in the doorway in order to block his way. Luckily, the phone on the wall behind her rang, taking her attention away from him.

Reaching the curtain, Ryder lifted a hand and pushed it aside. As he did so, he realized his restless boredom had disappeared, replaced by a sense of anticipation he hadn't felt in a long time.

Hannah heard the familiar rasp of the curtain rings sliding on the metal rod. She was bent over a thigh-high box, shoving handfuls of wood shavings out of her way so she could remove the contents. She had suggested to her suppliers that they use natural materials for packing instead of plastic, but the wood shavings were a nuisance. They stuck to her clothes and dispensed slivers of wood into her fingers when handled too much. She wouldn't complain, though, if the packing material had protected the contents of the box from breaking when she'd accidentally dropped it.

Assuming her clerk, Dayzie, had entered the back room and was about to lecture her on swearing where customers could hear her, she bent farther over the box. Her voice was muffled as she searched for a piece of pottery. "I know what you're going to say, Dayzie, but I had a good excuse for my bad language. You'd have cussed a blue streak, too, if this heavy box had landed on your foot."

"No doubt about it," agreed a distinctly masculine voice.

Hannah froze for a few seconds, then slowly, carefully, straightened and turned around. A man she'd never seen before stood just inside the curtained doorway. She saw his gaze slide over her, staring at her leather western boots, then gliding over her denim jeans before lingering briefly at the silver clasp on her brown leather belt and the silver bracelets on her right wrist. She placed her hands on her hips as he took in her vest, made out of outdated men's ties and worn over a white shirt.

She was aware that though her shirt had been crisp and fresh when she'd put it on that morning, it hadn't made it through the day that way. Now it was less than pristine, marred by vermilion-and-buff-colored dust, perspiration, and bits of wood shavings.

She wasn't ashamed of the fact she worked for a living, but she recognized the feminine regret that she wasn't looking her best in front of an attractive man.

When his thorough inspection reached her face, she was startled by the warmth flooding her cheeks as his gaze paused on her mouth. Good Lord, she thought with disgust. She was actually blushing like a thirteen-year-old girl being kissed for the first time.

She lowered her own gaze to his western boots, which were even more worn than hers, an indication that he wasn't a tourist who had recently removed the price tag from his new western clothes. On purpose, she allowed her examination of him to follow the same route his had taken. She hoped he was as irritated with her frank scrutiny as she'd been by his.

She, however, was not supposed to enjoy it.

Black denim clung to long legs and slim hips. She noticed he didn't wear a large belt buckle that proclaimed his taste in beer or his fondness for wildlife. Like her own clothing, his black shirt showed the effects of the hot, dry day, and he had undone several buttons at the neck. Unlike her, he wore a black felt hat with the brim pulled down in front, shadowing his eyes.

When he lifted his head a little, she met his

shaded gaze. His eyes were the color of the lapis lazuli stones she used occasionally when making jewelry. She had the unsettling feeling she would be reminded of this man every time she worked with lapis from now on.

She also noticed that those blue eyes were glittering with humor. He obviously found her thorough examination amusing instead of insulting. Several creased lines radiated outward from the corner of his eyes, caused either by squinting at the sun or from finding a great deal in life worth laughing at. Maybe it was a combination of both, she thought, as she noticed his deep tan.

It didn't bother her that she was obviously the cause of his amusement. She was able to laugh at herself and wasn't overly sensitive when others found her funny on occasion. What did annoy her was the way her heart rate was accelerating. She didn't find her reaction to this man remotely amusing. A heart attack would be easier to accept than being attracted to an Anglo.

She stared pointedly at his black hat. "Didn't your mother teach you that it's polite to take your hat off in front of a lady?"

He nodded. "And to open doors for them, pull out their chairs, and help them on with their coats."

"Think how upset she'd be if she knew you still have your hat on."

He crossed his arms over his chest. "She'd have been more horrified to hear a woman cussing a blue streak. Ladies aren't supposed to swear."

She tilted her head to one side as she considered his statement. "Not even if they drop a box of pottery on their foot?"

He shook his head, his amused gaze never leaving hers. "I don't know any lady who would try to emulate a stevedore by attempting to carry a box that size in the first place. Usually they're more than happy to let a big strong male do the heavy work."

"What if there isn't a man around?"

"They wait until a guy shows up or they leave the box where it is."

She shrugged. "You might as well leave your hat on, then. According to your definition, I don't qualify as a lady. If I had to stand around waiting for some man to come to my rescue, the crates would pile up to the ceiling."

He raised an eyebrow as if surprised by the stinging bite in her voice. "Maybe you haven't been asking the right man."

"Possibly," she said, her dry tone implying there was no such thing. "That seems to be a common complaint among most single women, doesn't it? Toting boxes isn't the only unladylike thing I do. I find it very satisfying to cuss when I do something stupid."

"You're very good at it. I learned a few interesting combinations of words I'll have to remember."

"You do that." She flicked a glance at his chest and upper arms. "Are those muscles for show, or do they really work?"

"They work," he answered, the creases at the corners of his eyes deepening. "Why?"

She gestured toward the box on the floor. "I need to move this shipment of pottery from here to over there." She pointed at a wooden shelf unit built into an outer wall some ten feet away.

He stepped toward her and the crate at her feet. "Do you usually put customers to work?"

Hannah was impressed at how easily he lifted the box and carried it to the shelf unit. As she followed him, she answered his question.

"Customers don't usually come into the storeroom. In the store, the customers are always right. Back here, I'm always right. But tell me, did you come back here to complain about my bad language or was there something you wanted?"

He set the box down and straightened, pushing his hat up an inch with the tip of a finger.

"Your picture doesn't do you justice."

She blinked. "What picture?"

"The one included in the geologist's report."

"What geologist's report?" She realized she sounded like a rather stupid parrot, but she was completely baffled by what he was saying.

"Your grandmother, Dawn Skylark, asked us to do preliminary tests three years ago to determine if she had any oil or copper on her land."

"And you're just now getting around to following up on the report?" she asked with more than a hint of skepticism. "The test results must have been terribly exciting for you to rush right over."

He smiled faintly at her sarcasm. "Timing is everything," he drawled. "I wasn't ready three years ago."

She didn't even pretend to understand what he was talking about. "Whatever that means," she murmured with a shrug. "You should have moved a little faster. My grandmother passed away six months ago."

"I know. And I'm sorry. From the report I read, she sounded like a unique woman. I would like to have met her."

"She was one of a kind," Hannah agreed. "I know this sounds rude, but could you get to the point? I have a lot of work to do."

"I'm Ryder Knight, owner of Wildcat Drilling out of Houston, Texas." He extended his right hand toward her. "I want to talk to you about leasing mineral rights to some of the property you inherited from Dawn Skylark."

Hannah stared at his hand with all the enthusiasm of someone about to touch a live poisonous snake, then clasped her fingers around his. Her silver bracelets clattered pleasantly as she shook his hand firmly but briefly. Her grandmother had taught her that a great deal could be learned about a person by his handshake. Ryder Knight's palm and fingers were callused, indicating he didn't spend all his time behind a desk. His grip was strong, yet gentle enough not to hurt her. He didn't force his strength on her, although she sensed he wanted her to be aware of it.

Her grandmother hadn't explained what it meant to feel an electric jolt at the touch of a man's hand, but an explanation hadn't been necessary. Hannah knew, and she instantly set out to make the attraction disappear, and Ryder Knight along with it. Breaking eye contact would be the first step.

Turning her back to him, she bent over the box and lifted out a decorated pottery vase with braided handles. "I hope you haven't made a long trip, Mr. Knight," she said as she brushed sawdust from the fired clay surface. "I won't allow my grandmother's land to be invaded by drill rigs."

"I can give you names of people to talk to," he answered readily, "who will tell you we don't tear up the land, landowners who have no complaints about the condition of their property after we've worked on it."

She set the vase on the shelf and bent over to retrieve another. "What about the people who do have complaints? Would you be willing to give me their names too?"

"The only complaints have been when we hit a dry hole."

Hannah lifted her gaze from the pot she'd taken out of the crate. His expression was the same, but she'd detected a note of defensive pride in his voice. Scrape a man's ego, she reminded herself, and he'd get sore.

"You're wasting your time and mine, Mr. Knight," she said, meeting his gaze squarely. "I won't give you what you want."

Ryder wondered what her reaction would be if he told her the lease wasn't all he wanted. Imagining how she would look without her clothes on was crowding out quite a few business details. With surprising difficulty, he pulled his tantalizing thoughts away from the physical and back to the practical.

"The sign outside of town said Bacon Ridge is the friendliest town in Arizona," he complained mildly. "You and everyone else I've run into since I arrived don't appear to have read that sign. I haven't seen any examples of warm hospitality since I got here. People look at me as though I'm carrying a disease."

"I wouldn't take it personally, Mr. Knight. There's been a rash of burglaries lately. Stealing from people who don't have much tends to make them cross and suspicious. They would rather blame strangers than think it's someone they know."

He raised a brow. "Do I look like a burglar?"

Hannah shook her head. "You look like trouble." She frowned as if puzzling over something, then asked, "Did you stop at the gas station at the other end of the street?"

"Yes," he answered, a world of caution in his voice. "Why?"

"Did you pay with cash or credit card?"

"I used the company credit card, as usual," he said with a touch of impatience. His scowl disappeared as he realized where she was going with her questions. "The station attendant read my company's name and spread the word that someone from a drilling company was in town."

She nodded. "Especially if it was Billy Chee

who waited on you. He's a walking information booth. All he had to do was phone Dayzie, who's working here, and she would whip up a news flash that a *bilagaana* from Wildcat Drilling is snooping around."

"A *bilagaana*?"

"Someone not Navajo," she explained. "Representing a drilling operation will make you less popular than being an Anglo or suspected of burglary. Some of our neighbors and relatives have been burned by speculators who promised a lot and delivered zip."

Ryder knew it happened. This wasn't the first time he'd run into prejudice caused by unscrupulous developers and drilling operations.

"I don't deal in promises or give guarantees. Nor do I cheat clients. If we're successful, everyone involved benefits. If we hit a dry hole, the landowner isn't out anything except having had my crew on his land temporarily."

She bent over to retrieve more pottery from the box. "I'm not interested, Mr. Knight. I hope you haven't come all the way from Houston because of a three-year-old survey. You'll have made a long trip for nothing."

He decided to try a different approach, one that usually persuaded landowners to sign on the dotted line. Most people had a price. He just had to find out what hers was. He mentioned an impressive sum of money he would pay for permission to drill on her land, then another amount she could expect if they came across valuable mineral deposits.

She whistled softly. "That's a lot of money," she said casually as she placed a piece of pottery next to the others.

Ryder wondered why he was disappointed that it was going to be this easy. "The more we find, the more you get. You wouldn't have to ever carry another heavy box. You would be a very wealthy woman."

She turned her head to look at him over her shoulder. "Wealth comes in many forms, Mr. Knight. Cold hard cash is only one of them." Her attention shifted to the curtained doorway. "It's all right, Dayzie. We won't need that."

Ryder glanced over his shoulder to see what Hannah meant and saw the clerk standing in the doorway, a shotgun held in her hands.

Both barrels were pointed at him.

The Navajo woman spoke to Hannah in her own language. Ryder had no idea what she said, but her tone of voice was unmistakable. She was not happy. The expression in the older woman's eyes when she darted a glance at him made it clear he was the major cause of her unhappiness.

When Hannah answered in the same language, her voice was soothing and patient. Whatever she told the clerk convinced the older woman that Hannah was in no need of her protection. The woman lowered the shotgun, scowled at Ryder for a few seconds, then swept aside the curtain and left the storeroom.

Ryder looked back at Hannah. "Does she treat all men like that, or am I the exception?"

"We had a break-in last week. Dayzie has been wary of strangers because of it. It doesn't help that she knows you represent a drilling company. I told her you would be leaving town soon."

Once more she turned her back to him to finish unpacking the shipment of pottery. He was being dismissed. Ryder stared at her with narrowed eyes as he debated with himself. To be a fool or not to be a fool, that was the question, he thought. It took him three seconds to decide. Playing it safe and sane had left him suffering from terminal boredom. Hannah Corbett might provide the cure. She was exotically beautiful and sensually exciting, and certainly not boring.

Closing the short distance between them, he took the glazed pot from her and put it on the shelf, ignoring the way she automatically resisted. "Why," he asked, "does your clerk think it was a stranger who broke in? Maybe the bad guy is someone who comes here all the time and decided to shop after hours."

"Not here. If it was someone from this area, they would steal food or cash, not Navajo rugs. They wouldn't take something most of them already have."

"That's all the burglar took? Just rugs?"

"The stolen rugs had price tags of several thousand dollars each," she explained. "I was going to ship them to a dealer in New York who pays cash on delivery instead of taking them on consignment. Now the weavers who spent over four hundred hours making the rugs are out the money they would have received from the sale."

"Four hundred hours?" he said in amazement. "To make a rug?"

She nodded. "That doesn't include the time it took to shear the sheep or spin and dye the wool. An average woven rug has thirty threads to the inch. High-quality Dineh rugs have around ninety. Some weavers say their rugs are woven so tightly, the weave could hold water and not leak a drop. They're worth every penny I can get for them."

"Dineh?" he repeated with a puzzled expression. "I've heard that word before."

"It means the People. Navajo."

"Is that the language you were speaking?"

"It was rude of me to talk to Dayzie in Athapascan in front of you, but she responds better in her own language." Hannah smiled faintly as she reminded him, "If you recall, she was holding a shotgun on you at the time. I thought being ill-mannered would be better than having to take you to the hospital—which is some distance away—to have a bullet removed from a part of your body you might consider important."

"I appreciate that," he drawled. "How did you learn to speak the Navajo language? One of my engineers who works mostly in Arizona thought that if he spoke their language, it would help in dealing with the men we occasionally hire from the reservation. He gave up after discovering how difficult it was to learn."

"Some English words don't have an equivalent in our language, which does make it difficult to learn. But did you have difficulty learning English when you were a child?"

"No more than anyone else," he said, and grinned. "Especially the swear words. I wasn't talking about English, though. I was referring to the complicated language you were speaking to Annie Oakley."

"It's not hard to learn if it's the only language you've heard as a child." Her smile was mocking, her eyes amused. "I thought you knew."

"Knew what?"

"I was raised on this land. My mother, her mother, and her mother were born here. Don't tell me the report you supposedly have doesn't mention the fact that my grandmother's property is Navajo land."

"It's not on the reservation," he pointed out. "When I did a follow-up on the report a couple of days ago, the title search revealed the property is in your name." He turned her words back on her. "You aren't going to try to tell me a woman with eyes the color of malachite is full-blooded Navajo?"

"My green eyes are courtesy of a man who stayed around long enough to make my mother pregnant," she said flatly. "He was an Anglo."

Obviously, she didn't expect any comment from him. She picked up the empty box and carried it to the other side of the storeroom.

Watching her walk away, Ryder realized she considered their conversation over. He didn't. He followed the same route she'd taken, around shelving units, cases of soft drinks, and cartons of canned goods, ending up gazing at her shapely backside. She was scooping the wood shavings out of the box into a large clear plastic bag. He saw her stiffen and hesitate, and he smiled. He hadn't made a sound when he'd approached, and she hadn't looked behind her. The only reason she'd known he was near her was that she was as aware of the attraction arcing between them as he was.

He put his hand on her shoulder, partly to get her to face him. He also wanted to test his reaction to touching her. And hers. When he felt the delicate bones through her cotton shirt, a sexual tension tightened his body with a ferocity that shocked him.

She didn't resist as the pressure of his hand turned her around. Standing straight and proud in front of him, she met his gaze unflinchingly, her expression defensive.

His voice was husky as he said, "See me tonight."

"No."

His fingers inadvertently tightened, and he made an effort to loosen his hold on her, his hand stroking her shoulder.

"Why not?" he asked quietly.

"What's the point? You'll try to persuade me to lease the mineral rights to you, and I'll keep refusing. It doesn't sound like much fun to me."

He met her gaze, his expression serious. "I'm not looking for fun, and I don't think you are either." He held his hand out, raising it so she could see the slight tremor in his fingers. "You have a strange effect on me, lady, and I'm not sure I like it. I don't know what the hell this is, but I'm going to find out." He ran a finger along the delicate line of her jaw. "We're both going to find out."

"You're wasting your time and mine, Mr. Knight," she said coldly. "My grandmother's land isn't available for exploitation, and neither am I."

Ryder was tempted to prove her wrong about his motives for wanting to see her later. The thought of how he could go about convincing her was making it difficult to think clearly; he was more accustomed to acting on his instincts. He had the feeling that kissing her was going to be more than he expected. And less than he wanted. He'd known her for approximately twenty minutes and already was wondering if her slender body would accept his, whether he would go out of his mind before or after he took her.

He dropped his hands so he was no longer touching her, feeling more ridiculous than he'd felt when he'd been a randy teenager with more hormones than good sense. She took a deep breath and let it out in a long sigh, and he wondered if she realized how much she was giving away.

"This is crazy," she said raggedly. "I've just met you."

His jaw clenched as he fought the need to touch her again, and he slid his hands into the back pockets of his jeans. It was the only thing he could think to do to prevent himself from reaching for her. Knowing she was experiencing her own response to him didn't do much for his self-control.

"I have a feeling," he murmured, "we're going to get to know each other very well, whether we like it or not."

Unable to resist, he pulled one hand from his pocket and ran the back of his forefinger down her cheek, over her jaw, and down the side of her neck. When he ran into the barrier of her collar, he dropped his hand, turned, and walked away.

As he disappeared beyond the curtain, Hannah let out the breath she'd been holding. She reached out to the nearest shelf for support, feeling oddly off-balance, as though she'd been on a runaway roller coaster and had been left excited, scared silly, and wary of ever riding it again.

TWO

Driving on the unpaved road had stirred up a cloud of dust, and Ryder coughed as some of it swirled in through the open side windows of his truck. When he reached a fork in the lane, he stopped, angling the truck so the relentless sun wouldn't shine directly on him. Not that it made all that much difference, he thought. It was still damn hot in the shade.

To his left, the lane led to a one-story out-building with a corral attached to the side and rear. Three horses were inside the fence. Ryder made a wild guess and decided that was the stables.

To the right, the lane ended at a small clap-board house that would have fit into the sitting room of his father's home in England, with some space left over. He guessed the house had two bedrooms, tops, maybe five small rooms in all. A building he'd learned was called a hogan, built of logs chinked with mud, was situated about twenty yards behind the house. The doorways of both dwellings opened to the east, which was traditional for Navajo dwellings, according to the owner of Tory's Cafe. Since Ryder had eaten all his meals at the cafe for the last two days, Tory himself had undertaken the chore of educating Ryder about the customs of the inhabitants of Bacon Ridge.

The cafe owner had even told Ryder how Bacon Ridge had gotten its name. It seemed that back in the late 1800s, an ambitious entrepreneur from the East had decided that Arizona was the perfect location to build a pork empire. Badly misinformed, the businessman sent a train-car full of pigs to an area he had bought for a pittance. The end result was a sad finality to his pork futures: When the source of water dried up in the summer, so did the pigs.

Ryder patiently listened to Tory's various tales, enjoying most of them, enduring others as he waited for the opportunity to slip in a question or two about Hannah.

Ryder smiled to himself. He'd discovered a great deal about local customs in general and Hannah Corbett in particular over the last couple of days. He'd developed an insatiable curiosity about the woman, along with a need to know why she'd made such an impression on him. His customary research on a landowner dealt in solid facts; he rarely indulged in gossip. In this case, though, he'd encouraged people to give him information about the owner of the Trading Post. Billy Chee had provided some of Hannah's background while working on the carburetor of Ryder's truck, and Tory had enlightened Ryder on a few facts over numerous cups of coffee. Ryder might not have known Hannah long, but he doubted if she'd have liked being the topic of conversation under either of those circumstances.

Nor would she have liked knowing she was the reason he was staying in town. The odd restlessness he'd been fighting for months had been replaced by his fascination with Hannah Corbett, and he knew he wouldn't be satisfied until he learned everything there was to know about her.

Dust boiled and churned on the road behind him. In his rearview mirror, he watched the dark spot in the center of the dun-colored cloud grow bigger until he could make out the contours of a Jeep and the face of the woman driving it. Her expression was as dark as the black hair whipping around her head. His blood heated at the wild, primitive picture she made, with the storm of dust whirling around her like an out-of-control cyclone.

He was familiar with his response. He'd been in a state of semi-arousal since he'd met her two days ago. Instead of diminishing, the attraction was growing stronger.

Ryder managed, barely, to contain a grin as Hannah drove past him without even slowing down, her high speed stirring the gritty sand violently. He got the impression she wasn't exactly thrilled to see him.

Coughing and squinting as he was engulfed by the dust cloud, he caught a glimpse of her Jeep turning onto the left fork of the road, heading toward the stables.

Ryder didn't start his truck to follow her. He'd come this far; now it was up to her to meet him halfway. Why that was important evaded him. He didn't want to analyze his motives yet. It was enough to recognize and act on them.

Hannah parked in her usual spot to one side of the closed stable doors, but didn't get out right away. Thanks to the active Bacon Ridge grapevine, she'd already known Ryder hadn't left town. When Billy Chee had walked into the Trading Post for his usual pack of chewing gum the previous morning, he'd mentioned that the wildcatter's travel trailer was parked on the empty lot behind the gas station. For a small fee, Ryder had been allowed to hook the trailer up to the station's electricity via a long extension cord.

For the past two days, every time Hannah had heard the bell over the door clang, she'd expected to see Ryder's tall frame. He hadn't come to the Trading Post, though, which made her more nervous than she would have been if he had shown up.

Bad news always traveled faster than good news, and she'd known that the town's animosity toward him had undergone a remarkable change. She got the impression Ryder had managed to win people over with his considerable charm. When they'd pinned him down to specific questions about his reasons for staying in Bacon Ridge, however, the people who'd been so free with answers about Hannah's life had received little information from Ryder concerning his.

She knew he'd been asking questions about her and getting answers, and she didn't like it. Each person who'd talked to Ryder swore to her that he or she hadn't told the stranger "anything important." Hannah couldn't be sure that was true, since she had no idea what he wanted to know.

She looked in her rearview mirror and caught the imposing image of the Bronco and the shadowed image of the man behind the wheel. Apparently, someone had let it slip where she lived. Either that, or the location had been included in the file he'd mentioned the first day he'd met her. Only a mile from the Trading Post, her grandmother's property was easy enough to find. It didn't matter how he'd found out—he was there now, and she was going to have to deal with him.

She'd done some research, too, and had found correspondence and references to phone calls in the files at the Trading Post dating back three years. Ryder had been right: Her grandmother had requested a survey from Wildcat Drilling. Hannah hadn't found anything that indicated Dawn Skylark had contacted any other company. Nor had she found any confirmation that the survey had been done, or what the results were if it was. A receipt was on file that showed the fee for the initial survey had been paid.

Hannah reached for the latch to open her door. She could take the easy way out and head directly toward her house rather than confront him, but she wouldn't. If she'd wanted her life to be smooth and predictable, she would have stayed in San Francisco. She'd known exactly what she was doing—what she was giving up and what she would gain—when she came back to Bacon Ridge. A tall, dark stranger hadn't figured in her expectations, however. Not someone like Ryder Knight, who reminded her she was a woman just by walking into a room.

With her head held high and the wind swirling her straight black hair around her, she walked toward Ryder's truck. As she'd been taught to do, she faced the problem head-on.

Ryder watched every step she took, unable to do a thing about his racing heartbeat. Today she was wearing white jeans with a coral cotton shirt tied at her waist. He caught a glimpse of a white tank top underneath the shirt and a necklace made of multiple strings of coral beads mixed with silver disks the size of a dime. A matching bracelet had been added to the assortment of silver bangles on her wrist. Thick hoop earrings the size of silver dollars could be seen against the dark curtain of her hair.

The defiant tilt of her chin was a challenge he was more than willing to take on. Ryder was more determined than ever to find out why he was reacting to her like a helpless moth attracted to a deadly flame. Losing control of his sexual urges at his age would be extremely foolish and possibly dangerous, he reminded himself. The sensible side of his mind, however, was outvoted by a more basic urge.

He wanted her, and he was going to have her.

She stopped near the driver's side of his Bronco and smiled faintly. "I suppose it's too much to hope that you've taken a couple of wrong turns and are lost."

He shook his head slowly. "I know what I'm doing and why."

"That makes one of us. I'm at a complete loss." She changed the subject, but the guarded expression in her eyes remained. "If you promise not to start badgering me about the mineral rights, I'll invite you inside and give you something cool to drink."

He shoved on his hat, unlatched the door, and waited for her to step back before pushing it open. When she finally did, he ducked his head in order to clear the cab of the truck. The sound of a horse whinnying came from the corral as he fell into step beside her.

Shortening his stride to hers, he asked, "How many horses do you have?"

"You mean you don't know?" she asked with mock surprise. "After drilling the population of Bacon Ridge for the past couple of days, I would have thought you wouldn't need to ask that question."

"I must be slipping," he drawled. "The amount of livestock you own never came up."

"Dear me. We can't have that now, can we? I

have three horses. My grandmother used to have a string of fifteen when she raised sheep. When I turned the herds over to the Bacon Ridge Cooperative, I sold the other horses, too, since I didn't have a use for them or anyone except myself to take care of them."

"Is that why you didn't keep the sheep? Because you couldn't take care of them?"

"That's part of the reason. I couldn't take care of the stock and run the Trading Post too. My grandmother had use for the sheep, spinning their wool into yarn for rugs. She had the time to move them to different grazing areas too. I couldn't be in two places at once."

Ryder wondered for a moment if that was regret he heard in her voice, then said, "My older brother Michael has a ranch in Montana where he raises quarter horses. He hates to sell off any of the colts, but that's the business he's in, so he does it." He looked down at the woman walking beside him. "We tease him that the woman who eventually marries him will have to have good bloodlines, a healthy coat, and all of her teeth."

"We?" Hannah asked as she stepped onto the flagstone path leading to her front door.

"There are four of us. I have another brother, Turner, and a younger sister, Silver."

"Silver Knight," she murmured. "I imagine she's endured a lot of teasing about her name."

He chuckled. "Having three older brothers taught Silver to attack first rather than wait to defend herself. No one makes fun of her or her name without wishing they hadn't."

"You left out your famous father," she added casually as she opened the front door. "From what I've read about him, King Knight wouldn't be an easy person to ignore."

Ryder didn't immediately follow her inside. Her announcement had stopped him in his tracks. He'd underestimated Hannah Corbett. While he'd been looking into her background, she'd been checking out his!

She was smart, he thought. And sneaky. Smiling to himself, he pushed open the door. Damned if he wasn't intrigued to find a woman with those particular qualities.

It took his eyes a few seconds to adjust to the dim room after the brightness outside. Drapes were pulled over the windows in the living room to keep out the hot rays of the sun, but that also eliminated a lot of light.

He removed his hat and hooked it over one of the stubby branches of a wooden hall tree to the left of the front door. More out of habit than a conscious effort to tidy his appearance, he combed his fingers through his sweat-dampened hair as he glanced around the living room.

The furniture was serviceable rather than any particular style. A wood-framed sofa and a matching chair had seat cushions with deep indentations, silently attesting to the extent of wear and tear they had endured over the years. The upholstered furniture was covered with a faded material depicting prancing deer, trees, and birds in muted browns and greens.

His sister had once told Ryder, in blunt sisterly fashion, that he had the fashion sense of a stuffed zucchini. Especially when he had dared to criticize her penchant for bright colors, which flowed from her closet to her apartment furnishings to her little red sports car. Silver might be right about his tastes, but his first impression of Hannah's place was that this wasn't her home; it was still her grandmother's. Hannah obviously slept there, but he couldn't see a single thing that indicated she had made any impression on the room. He saw signs of her grandmother's previous occupancy: a shawl spread over the back of a chair, wire-rimmed half glasses resting on top of a sewing basket.

Hannah's voice interrupted his perusal. "If you'd like to sit down," she said, "I recommend the far end of the sofa. The springs are tired everywhere else and might do you bodily harm. The chair will sort of swallow you as you sink into the cushions. It's a challenge to get up again. I'll be back in a few minutes."

While he waited for her to return, Ryder tried to figure out where the humble cabin fit in with the constantly changing picture of Hannah Corbett in his mind.

One of the things he'd discovered about her was that she had left her teaching job in San Francisco in order to return to Bacon Ridge and take care of Dawn Skylark when she fell ill. Hannah's mother had died when Hannah was four, and her grandmother had raised her. The owner of the cafe, who'd shared this information, seemed to consider Hannah's sacrifice unremarkable. Ryder got the impression from Tory that Hannah had only been doing what was expected of her. Ryder didn't have any problem with a woman caring for a loved one; the fact that Hannah had stayed after her grandmother died was the part Ryder was having trouble understanding. It was like using a jackhammer to crack an egg. Hannah was overqualified to be running a general store in a remote small town. With her education, she would have no problems finding a teaching position anywhere there was a vacancy.

Why did she stay? he wondered, not for the

first time. Why did she work so damn hard at the Trading Post, especially when he'd discovered that she gave many of the store's goods away in the guise of issuing credit?

Why in hell did it matter to him what she did?"

Perspiration trickled down his chest. The room was only marginally cooler than outside. The Trading Post and the restaurant had air-conditioning, but it was obvious Hannah didn't have any cooling system in her home, not even a fan to swirl the hot air around. Since the only lamps he could see were filled with kerosene, he concluded the house wasn't wired for electricity.

To take his mind off the oppressive heat, he walked over to a wall where a number of framed photographs and several faded blue ribbons were hanging. A bookcase and a small desk were below them, and trophies of all sizes and shapes took up most of the space on the shelves and on top of the desk. Looking closer, Ryder saw that the engraved plates all had Hannah's name on them, along with a date and the rodeo event she had entered.

He leaned forward to examine a photo showing a younger Hannah participating in a barrel race in a rodeo. He guessed her age to be about thirteen or fourteen. Having been around horses all of his life, he was able to appreciate how comfortable she appeared on the back of one. He'd seen only one other person ride as though he were part of the horse, and that was his brother Michael.

He turned as he heard her walk back into the room. She was carrying two long-necked bottles of cola, and moisture had collected on the glass, proof that the contents were cold.

"Thanks," he said as she handed him one, then took several long swallows.

"Hmmm," he murmured. "I'm glad I was wrong in assuming you don't have electricity."

"You weren't wrong. I bought a portable generator when I came back from San Francisco. Luckily, my grandmother's land is close enough to town to have water hooked up, although she had to pay for the pipes to be installed out here." She tilted her head to one side, grinning crookedly. "I'm surprised you didn't already know that either."

"Obviously there are several gaps in the grapevine." He glanced at the trophies and ribbons. "For instance, no one mentioned you were a rodeo star."

Her gaze shifted briefly to the pictures hanging above the trophies. "My grandmother didn't like it when I entered rodeo events, but as you can see, she kept all the newspaper articles that had my name listed, along with the ribbons and trophies I won over the years."

He directed the tip of his bottle toward the photo he'd been examining earlier. "You look like you've having a good time."

She leaned closer to look at the picture, then met his gaze, grinning. "I beat Nessa Turnhill that day, and she had to give me her most prized possession, a napkin autographed by Buster Eaglefeather. It was our own private wager before the race."

"Who's Buster Eaglefeather?"

"He was the number one rodeo broncobuster at the time and every young girl's dream. He was drop-dead gorgeous, with an eagle feather tattooed on his arm and a way of walking that would make an angel blush."

"Hot stuff," Ryder drawled. His gaze flicked from her to the photos, and back to her. "Rodeo rider, schoolteacher, businesswoman. You definitely have a wide variety of interests. Do they include eating?"

"You've been busy," she murmured, ignoring his question. "Who told you about the teaching degree?"

"Billy Chee at the gas station," he said easily, enjoying the irritation he saw in her eyes. He wondered if she was aware that her Native American heritage was most apparent when she was angry. She looked as proud and defiant as any warrior. "He mentioned you were teaching adults to read while you wait for an opening at the community college in Many Farms. Some of the patrons of the restaurant mentioned you'd been away for four years teaching in California and came back when your grandmother became ill. And that after she died, you stayed on."

"I suppose being talked about over a couple of gas pumps and cups of coffee is better than being whispered about over a beer at a local bar. I can't say I like it much, though."

"I didn't think you would."

"But knowing I wouldn't like people gossiping about me didn't stop you from listening to whatever they had to say."

"Something like that."

She brushed her finger over the bottle in her hand, catching the moisture on the glass. "As much as Billy likes to talk, I can't see him volunteering my life's story on his own. That means you asked him about me. Why?"

"I think that's obvious. I wanted to know more about you."

"Why?"

A corner of his mouth curved upward. "For

the same reason you did a background check on me—curiosity."

She shook her head. "The only reason I made a few inquiries about you was so I would know who I was dealing with. Call it a woman's intuition or an educated guess, but I had a feeling you don't give up easily."

"Always go with your instincts. I do. You didn't answer my question: Do you include eating among your many interests?"

"I'm not going out with you, Mr. Knight," she said firmly.

"Ryder," he interjected.

Hannah figured she could be stubborn and continue to use formality as a barrier, but she knew him well enough already to know he would just batter it down.

"My answer is the same, Ryder. I don't have time for a social life."

"I'm not suggesting a ladies' tea. I was thinking more along the lines of a thick steak and a fresh salad."

"Even if I liked the idea, which I don't," she lied, "I wouldn't be able to go. I have too many things to do—a lesson plan to go over, papers to correct from the adult reading class, horses to feed, and book work for the Trading Post."

"Would the world come to an end if one of those chores didn't get done tonight?"

"Probably not, but whatever doesn't get done tonight would have to be squeezed into tomorrow, which already has a full schedule."

"You have to eat sometime," he said reasonably.

"I'll grab a sandwich after I bring the horses into the stables for the night and feed them."

He considered her answer for thirty seconds, then nodded. "All right."

The heels of his boots rang loudly in the quiet house as he walked over to the hall tree. He lifted his hat off it and settled it on his head, the brim low.

With one hand on the doorknob, he looked back at her. "Aren't you coming with me?"

"Didn't you hear a word I said? I'm not going out with you."

"I thought you were in such a hurry to get your chores done."

"I'll do them after you leave."

"Aw, well, that would delay the chores, Hannah, since I'm not leaving."

"You have a definite problem with your hearing," she said with growing exasperation. "I told you I have things to do tonight, and they don't include arguing with you about mineral rights."

"There's nothing wrong with my hearing. You came through loud and clear." He opened the door. "I'm going to help you. You'll get finished quicker."

She opened her mouth to protest, but he forestalled her. "We'll get done twice as fast," he said, grinning, "and then you'll have more time to argue with me."

Hannah forgot to be irritated when the possibilities of the kind of help he could give her in the stables ran through her mind. Cleaning out the stalls was usually a project she saved for the weekends. For Ryder Knight, she would make an exception.

She smiled up at him as she walked past him, out the door. "How do you feel about manure?"

"I can take it or leave it," Ryder answered, not too sure he was going to like where her question was leading. He was also suspicious about her smile.

The wind blew a thick strand of her hair across his chest as they walked toward the stable. He looked down at the strand of black silk as it seemed to writhe across his shirt. He didn't trust himself to touch her hair. His arousal was beating hot and hard against the zipper of his jeans, and all she'd done was smile at him. It wouldn't take much to ignore all the warnings he'd posted deep inside his consciousness about getting involved. He'd decided a long time ago that a wildcatter could move around more easily alone, without dragging someone along with him.

Every male instinct he possessed warned him this was one woman he would have a difficult time walking away from.

"How about shoveling manure?" she asked with a teasing gleam in her eyes.

"If you ask the right people," he muttered, "they'll tell you I can spread it around with the best of them."

Her laughter competed with the wind. "And you don't even need a pitchfork."

She'd tilted her head back to glance up at him, and his breath caught in his throat. Golden lights of humor were glimmering in her eyes, and the sun was glowing on her golden skin. As badly as he wanted to reach out and pull her into his arms, he fought the desire slashing through him.

He shifted his gaze away from her, concentrating on the stables and the corral beyond. "I should be thankful you don't still have sheep. You'd be tempted to have me clip their wool."

"That would be overkill," she said, the humor

still apparent in her voice. "Cleaning out the stalls will do nicely."

He tugged at one of the large doors while she pulled open the other one. "Is shoveling manure some kind of Navajo courtship ritual?"

Her head snapped around. "Courtship? Where did that come from? The only reason you're here is to try to persuade me to give you permission to drill on my grandmother's land. Helping me with the horses is your way of softening me up."

"That's part of it," he admitted. "The other part is I want to help you with your work so you can finish faster. I'm hungry."

He had to lift the door an inch or so for it to swing open. The hinges needed to be tightened so the bottom would clear the hard-packed ground. The stable door was only one of the things he'd noticed needed repairing.

"Don't you have any help around here?" he asked. "There's enough work for at least two men to stay busy for a month."

"Or two women."

"Or two women," he conceded.

"And no," she went on, "I don't have any help. I don't need it."

Knowing he didn't have a right to interfere by

giving advice didn't stop him. There were many ways of becoming involved in another person's life that had nothing to do with sex, and just because he had difficulty thinking of anything *but* sex when he was with her didn't mean he couldn't try to concentrate on assisting her.

He made the mistake of looking at her and almost groaned aloud. She was standing with her feet slightly apart, her hands on her hips. The air around her practically crackled with the pride and fire emanating from her. He wasn't sure how much longer he could wait to tap into that magnificent life within her.

She would probably slug him if he even so much as kissed her, he decided—but damn if he didn't think it might be worth it.

"That's tough," he muttered.

"What?"

"I said that's tough if you don't think you need any help, because you're getting it. Go do your book work, and I'll take care of the horses. Then we'll fix something to eat, and you can yell at me some more. Now is not a good time."

"Why not? Maybe if I keep arguing with you, you'll get fed up and leave."

"Not a chance." He took a step toward her. Then another. Three feet of Arizona soil was all that stood between them. "If you stay out here with me, Hannah, there isn't a chance in hell I'll be able to keep my hands off you. So which is it going to be?"

She didn't give him an answer right away. Her eyes seemed to change to a darker green, their expression unreadable as she stared up at him.

Ryder felt as though he was being assessed, weighed, and judged on an invisible scale. He would have given a great deal to know what she was thinking.

"What do you know about horses?" she asked.

"Enough to know which end needs feeding and which end makes the mess in the stalls. I grew up with horses in Kentucky and in England after my parents moved there. And my brother raises horses on his ranch in Montana, remember? When I visit him, he puts me to work. I won't do myself or the horses any bodily harm with a pitch-fork."

Apparently satisfied he wasn't a complete amateur, she gave him brief instructions, then walked back to the house.

Ryder allowed himself the luxury of watching her until she disappeared inside. He might have spoken too hastily about not doing harm with the pitchfork, he realized. If he didn't get his mind off wondering how she would taste, he was as likely to stab his foot as a bale of straw.

Almost without thinking, he shoved a hand into the front pocket of his jeans and took out the cash receipt from lunch. His fingers nimbly folded the paper, bent it back, then folded it again a number of times until the form of a frog developed. He examined the little creature he'd made. In the fairy tale, the frog changed into a prince after the princess kissed him.

He wouldn't magically turn from a Knight into a prince if he kissed Hannah, but he had a strong feeling he would be changed forever.

The small table in Hannah's bedroom was piled high on one end with spelling papers to be corrected and lesson plans for her adult class. She wasn't making much progress on either stack.

With the tip of her forefinger, she traced the initials she'd gouged into the wooden tabletop with a ballpoint pen years ago when she was supposed to be doing homework. The multiple coats of paint her grandmother had applied over the years had almost obliterated the letters, but Hannah knew they were there.

The table was like everything else in her grandmother's house: old, worn, and in need of replacement. Furniture was way down the list of things she had to take care of, however. Her now-depleted savings had made a sizable dent in the tax debt she had inherited along with the land. The extension she'd been granted gave her a little over eight months to come up with the rest. It was a daunting total to raise, but not impossible.

Except that she wasn't able to save much of her income from the Trading Post when she kept extending credit to so many customers. She hoped the sale of the silver jewelry she was learning to make would cover the loss.

She pushed back her chair and stood up. Walking over to the window, she looked toward the stables. The horses were no longer in the corral, so Ryder had apparently managed to get them inside. Evidently, he had more experience with horses than he'd let on. One of her horses, Juniper, was often stubborn about entering the stables. Either he'd caught Juniper on a cooperative day or Ryder's charm didn't extend only to people.

She bit her bottom lip as she thought about the reason he had come to Bacon Ridge. She wished he hadn't quoted such a high price for the mineral rights that first day. The money he'd offered would clear the tax debt with enough left over to fix up the house, repair the roof on the stable, and have electricity installed.

Accepting the fee would cause other problems, however, and she had enough to cope with at the moment.

The sun was almost below the horizon, but it was too early for the air to lose its heat. The shiver that ran over her skin when she thought of Ryder was caused by an inner chill of apprehension. Excitement and desire made her nerve endings feel as though she'd touched a live electrical wire. In the past, she'd thought she knew what sexual desire was and how it felt. Now she realized she'd had only a small glimpse of the real thing.

When she'd seen Ryder standing in the doorway of the storeroom, she'd had one of those rare moments of premonition. An instinct had warned her that the tall stranger would be responsible for major changes in her life. After that first meeting, she'd tried to tell herself she'd been imagining things. She'd been almost convinced, until she'd walked up to his truck that evening and seen the blue fire in his eyes.

Hannah rubbed her arms, hoping to bring some warmth back to her skin as she recalled how her body had responded to the sensual blaze in his gaze. He'd been more honest than she, she admitted. Denying her attraction wouldn't make it go away. Giving in to it, however, would be the most foolish thing she'd ever done.

Hadn't she learned anything from what happened to her mother?

Over the years, her grandmother had taught her that many things could not be changed by man. A person's destiny was one of them. Fighting the designs of Mother Earth and Father Sky was useless and could be painful.

Hannah's gaze was drawn back to the stable doors as Ryder stepped out of the dark interior and closed first one door, then the other. His long strides covered the ground quickly as he headed for the cabin, and she watched, mesmerized by his natural male grace.

When he was close enough to spot her at the window, she turned away. Maybe she couldn't change fate, but she could delay it. She needed time to think, to plan, and it was up to her to ensure she had it. She couldn't afford to make a mistake, and she didn't mean financially.

She stepped outside as Ryder approached the house. Closing the door behind her, she asked, "Did you have any problems?"

He stopped a couple of feet away from her. "Your horses are tucked in for the night. All fed and groomed, with the cleanest stalls in town."

She held out her right hand. "Thank you."

He glanced down at her hand, but didn't take it. As he raised his gaze to meet hers, a smile softened the hard line of his mouth. "I shouldn't have given you so much time alone, should I? You've managed to talk yourself into playing it safe by getting rid of me."

"You can believe whatever you want," she said lightly, as though it didn't matter. "I meant what I said about having work to do."

Ryder chose that moment to take her hand, then enjoyed her quick intake of breath as his fingers wrapped around hers. Instead of completing a handshake, he stroked the back of her hand with his thumb.

"You're only delaying the inevitable, Hannah," he said softly. "I'm not blind. You're as attracted to me as I am to you."

She didn't try to pull her hand away, but her eyes were cold enough to give frostbite.

"I don't fall into bed with every man I'm attracted to, Ryder. If I've given you that impression, it wasn't intentional."

"I don't usually want to sleep with a woman I've just met, either. You're the exception."

"Gee, thanks," she said. "You're going to have to put this trip down as another 'dry hole,' wildcatter. I'm not now, tomorrow, or six months from now interested in having my grandmother's land violated. Nor am I available to show a cowboy passing through town a good time. If you'll let go of my hand, I'll get back to grading papers, and you can go on to your next venture."

Ryder had every intention of pushing harder for what he wanted, until he saw the shadows in her eyes. He couldn't deny the desire to take on her demons as his own, whatever they were, but at the moment, it appeared he was the demon.

Growing up with a younger sister had taught him that timing was very important in dealing with a female. This wasn't the time to press Hannah any further.

He smiled slowly as his gaze lowered to her lips. He would do as she asked, for now, but he'd be damned if he would go without a consolation prize.

"If you're going to kiss me off," he muttered, "at least you could do it properly."

He was certain she wasn't aware of the sudden flare of desire in her eyes, but he responded to that sensual warmth and ignored the wariness stiffening her spine. Lowering his head, he took her mouth with a demanding claim, as though she was already his. Hunger clawed in his gut and need writhed and coiled inside him. She tasted of every fantasy he'd ever had as a boy and as a man, and he greedily took as much as she was willing to give him.

He nearly lost it when she made a soft sound of pleasure and rose up on her toes to get closer to him, her arms sliding around his neck. The feel of her breasts pressing into his chest made him groan, a groan that ended abruptly with the shock of feeling her slender hips nudge his hard body.

When he realized how close he was to pulling her down onto the ground, he reluctantly eased away from her. Averting his gaze, he stared over her head while he waited to get his raging hunger under control. He didn't dare look at her. It would take more than he was capable of to withstand the passion warming her eyes. Lord knows, he'd felt it coming from her in waves when he'd held her in his arms.

Realizing he would never be fully in control so long as he was with her, he turned away and walked toward his truck without saying a word.

Hannah was tempted to dash inside, but she made herself watch him as he swung up into the cab of his Bronco. As he drove away and the rolls of dust eventually hid his vehicle from view, she closed her eyes to calm her breathing and the rampant beat of her heart.

He'd be back, she knew. Not only for the drilling rights, but for her. She had to decide what she was going to do when she saw him again, because she was pretty sure she knew what he would do.

THREE

Hannah tugged the long sleeve of her tan cotton shirt over the white gauze bandage around her wrist when she saw Ryder leaning against the outside wall of the Trading Post. It had been three days since she'd seen him, but the memory of his mouth covering hers had rarely left her thoughts while she'd been away.

She could tell by the narrowing of his eyes that her attempt to hide her injury was a few seconds too slow. He'd seen the bandage. The tight line of his mouth and his glowering gaze gave her the impression he was in a bad mood. Her own wasn't all that great either. Their combined attitudes wouldn't make for a cheerful conversation, but it looked like it couldn't be avoided.

She walked up the steps, her blue denim skirt dancing against the sides of her calf-high leather boots, and smiled politely. "Good morning, Mr. Knight. I thought you would have returned to Houston by now."

Ryder pushed away from the wall and walked toward her. He had to step around a few people loitering on the porch, then he was directly in front of her, blocking her path.

His voice was hard, quiet, and furious. "Where in hell have you been the last three days?"

"It's nice to see you again too," she said dryly.

"Don't give me the socially polite chitchat, Hannah. I'm not in the mood."

"I can see that."

"I want to know where you disappeared to for the past three days."

She raised a brow. His belligerent attitude was beginning to annoy her. "What makes you think it's any of your business?"

He took her arm when she attempted to step around him. "I'm making it my business, dammit. I've been going crazy worrying about you."

After several attempts, she gave up trying to pull away from him. She didn't stand a chance physically. That only left a verbal defense.

"I think 'crazy' is the operative word here." She kept her voice low so no one else could hear her, but she couldn't control the throbbing anger, which managed to get through loud and clear. "You have completely lost your mind, and I don't have the time to help you look for it. I don't remember assigning you as my keeper. Where I go and what I do has nothing to do with you."

Gripping Hannah's upper arms, Ryder lifted her up until her face was only inches away from his. "It wouldn't bother me one bit to show you why I have a right to worry about you, especially when you come back with a bandage on your arm." He brought her even closer, his eyes flashing fire. Lowering his voice for her ears only, he added, "What you need to worry about is whether I can kiss you and stop there."

Her eyes widened in shock and with the soul-deep arousal that hadn't dissipated even when she was miles away. She didn't doubt for a second that Ryder would do what he threatened, regardless of an audience. It wasn't easy for her to admit, even to herself, how badly she wanted him to take the decision away from her. Considering the hell her mother had suffered, Hannah was shocked by the direction her thoughts had gone so quickly.

An amused voice spoke behind her before she could think of a response. "What do you call this approach, Ryder? The Neanderthal method?"

Ryder dragged his gaze away from Hannah's mouth. When he recognized the man standing several feet away, he said in surprise, "Joe Underhill."

"Very good," the other man said lightly. He was as tall as Ryder, with a more muscular build. When he smiled, which was a great deal of the time, his teeth were a startling white in comparison to his deeply bronzed skin. His dark eyes weren't amused, however, as he glanced around at the crowd gathering and edging closer.

Still holding Hannah, Ryder stared at the dark-haired man. "Good Lord, how many years has it been?"

"Too many. I think you'd better let Hannah stand on her own two feet, Ryder. You evidently haven't noticed that you're about to find out how Custer felt at the Little Bighorn. You're definitely outnumbered."

Ryder was puzzled by the quiet warning, until he looked around. He and Hannah were surrounded by eight men of varying ages and sizes, all of whom were old enough, tough enough, and big enough to make an impression. None of them looked as though they would have any problems in breaking whatever part of his body they chose, or would even hesitate. Since their glares were directed at him, Ryder came to the conclusion that the men were cranky because he had his hands on Hannah.

He lowered Hannah so she was standing on the step below him. He didn't like releasing her, but it didn't look as if he had a choice.

Hannah used her freedom to turn and step down to the street, where Joe was standing. Ryder followed her. She looked from one man to the other and asked in an incredulous voice, "You two know each other?"

Joe grinned. "I was about to ask you the same thing. Ryder's lousy luck at cards helped pay my way through college. I often wondered if he lost on purpose 'cause he knew I needed the money."

Ryder stepped around Hannah, placing his left hand possessively on her shoulder as he leaned forward and held out his right hand. "You were the only one who could keep the engine running on my first oil rig." Shaking Joe's hand, he complained, "I had to buy a new rig when you left."

Joe gripped Ryder's hand tightly and briefly. When he released it, Joe looked at the men still standing around them. They'd relaxed their guard a bit, but not enough. Joe spoke a number of words that were incomprehensible to Ryder, but not to Hannah.

Ryder could feel her stiffen under his hand. Lowering his head so his mouth was near her ear, he asked, "What did he say?"

She turned her head, her lips only a breath

away from his. "He said you are a friend, a good friend who would not hurt me."

"That's true so far. What else did he say?"

She raised her gaze to meet his. "You are to be treated like a brother."

Chuckling, he murmured, "That's all right for Joe, honey, but not for you."

The men backed off, but Ryder noticed they remained in sight. A couple leaned against one of the hitching posts, a few stood near a truck in full view, others took up positions on the porch of the Trading Post. Just in case additional reinforcements were necessary, Dayzie, her trusty shotgun clenched in both hands, filled the doorway of the Trading Post.

Ryder shook his head and brought his amused gaze back to Joe. "A man could become paranoid around here."

"They are wary of strangers, especially around our women," Joe replied as he took Hannah's arm. "Let's go get a cup of coffee at the cafe. While you're filling me in on what you've been doing the last couple of years, everyone will see me with you and Hannah and relax."

Ryder fell into step on Hannah's other side. "Is that wedding ring on your left hand the real thing?" he asked Joe.

"It's very real. I married Hannah's best

friend, Nora Singer, when I graduated from college."

"Then you can let Hannah walk without your hand on her arm."

Ryder had spoken so casually, it took a few seconds for Joe to realize he was being warned off. He grinned as he made an exaggerated motion of releasing Hannah's arm. "I'll be damned," he muttered.

Hannah could have explained to Joe that any claim Ryder thought he had on her was only in his imagination. She wondered why she remained silent.

The table Joe chose in the cafe was in the middle of the room, even though several booths along the windows—which Ryder would have preferred—were empty. Ryder understood Joe's reasons for wanting them center stage, but he didn't like being on display. As a rule, he didn't care what people thought. In this case, though, Joe was protecting Hannah's reputation, so Ryder would put up with being the center of attraction for a little while. Like Joe and Hannah, he pretended not to see the curious glances being aimed in their direction.

He waited until they were all seated before he said, "Hannah, why don't you tell Joe what happened to your arm and where you've been the last three days. I'm sure he'd be interested. I am."

Hannah leaned back in her chair and smiled. "I'd rather find out how you two happen to know each other."

Joe glanced at the waitress behind the counter and held up three fingers. When the girl nodded, he looked at Hannah. "I have Dawn Skylark to thank for meeting Ryder. It was her idea I go work for him."

"My grandmother?" Hannah asked, shock widening her eyes. "She didn't contact Wildcat Drilling until three years ago. How could she have recommended Ryder's company before then?"

Joe crossed his arms over his chest and looked down his chiseled nose at her. "If your grandmother wanted you to know, she would have told you."

Hannah bristled. "Don't put on that 'stoic cigar-store Indian' act with me, Joe Underhill. It's not too late for me to tell Nora who stole her clothes when she and I went skinny-dipping in Singer Canyon."

"You wouldn't."

"I would."

Joe dropped his arms. "That's blackmail."

"That's right," she said with a grin. "Nora

would still like to get her hands on the person responsible for making her ride back home with a scratchy horse blanket wrapped around her instead of her clothes. Just think what she would do when she found out her own husband was the guilty party."

"We weren't married then."

"I don't think that will make a difference. You'll still be sleeping in the barn for a few days when she finds out."

Joe turned to Ryder. "You can jump in here anytime, you know."

"Not me. I'm as curious as Hannah about how you came to work for me. I thought you answered an ad I'd put in the paper. I never met Hannah's grandmother. I didn't even know her name until last week when I found her file on my desk. Why would Dawn Skylark send you to work for me?"

Indecision flickered in Joe's dark eyes, and then he said, "I guess it doesn't matter any longer."

Ryder and Hannah answered at the same time, in impatient tones. "What doesn't matter?"

Giving each of them a disgusted look, Joe said, "Geez, if that isn't gratitude for you. I should have minded my own business and let those men drag you out of town. See if I ever—"

Ryder and Hannah again spoke in unison, saying Joe's name in a similar warning tone.

"All right," he said with a martyred sigh.

The waitress approached their table. Her bright Hawaiian print smock was at least three sizes too big and was sliding off one shoulder. Since she was balancing two cups and saucers in one hand and a third in her other, she couldn't tug the shirt back in place. Luckily, she was wearing a pink uniform underneath. She handed out the steaming cups of coffee like she was dealing cards.

Hannah studied the shirt, shaking her head. "If Tory's going to make you wear those shirts, Donna, he could at least provide one that fits."

"Real stylish, aren't I?" The waitress hitched up her shoulder, but the shirt fell right back where it had been. Donna lowered her voice. "Tory's wife said he got this great deal on these shirts when they stopped at a gift shop off some alley on Maui. Trouble was, they only came in one size. Extra-large."

"Sounds like Tory," Joe said. "I need cream, Donna."

"No problem." The waitress dashed to the counter and dashed back, passing a handful of small containers to Joe. "Anything else?" she asked, but then moved on to another table before anyone had a chance to answer.

Joe took his time opening several plastic thimbles of cream, then slowly pouring their contents into his coffee. When he looked up, he saw that Hannah was offering him the sugar and Ryder was holding out a spoon to hurry him along.

Grinning, he accepted both. He poured sugar into his cup and then, while stirring the sweet, creamy coffee, began his story.

"I wanted to be a teacher ever since I opened my first book. My family didn't have the money to send me to college, and there weren't any jobs around here that would have paid enough for my tuition, even if I worked twenty-four hours a day all summer. The night before I was going to enlist in the Army, which I thought was the only option I had, Dawn Skylark came to see my mother. She said she was hoping I could help her by doing a favor for a friend instead of going into the military right away. By my helping this person, I'd also be able to earn enough money to start college in the fall and maybe not have to go in the military at all."

"Who was the friend?" asked Hannah.

Joe looked at Ryder. "King Knight."

Ryder and Hannah's reactions were almost identical.

"King?"

"Ryder's father?"

"My father?"

"You're crazy," Hannah announced. "My grandmother didn't know Ryder's father."

"They met when King was young. Dawn Skylark knew King's mother for a long time before that. They went back a long way." Joe held up his hand before they could start their chorus of disbelief again. "I don't know all the details. I heard something about King's older brother being a real hell-raiser when he was young and foolish. His mother—your grandmother, Ryder—sent him out to learn a few basics of life from her friend Dawn Skylark. The two women had gone to school together years before and had been friends ever since."

Hannah turned to Ryder, who looked as shocked as she felt. "Did you know this?"

He shook his head slowly. "I remember King mentioned something about his mother having gone to a boarding school while her parents were in Egypt digging up pyramids. I don't recall him saying exactly where his mother attended school."

Hannah dredged up her own memories. "I remember seeing a picture of my grandmother taken when she was very young. She and an Anglo girl who had to be about ten years old were standing with their arms around each other.

When I asked her who the other girl in the photo was, she said the girl was her sister. I asked her how that could be—she was an only child, and the girl in the photo wasn't Navajo. My grandmother told me of the first day she arrived at the boarding school where her family had sent her. People who spoke a strange language were going to cut off all her hair and wash her in kerosene to get rid of any lice she might have. An Anglo girl stopped them. My grandmother made a sign with her hands to describe what happened."

Hannah pointed at her left cheek with her right index finger, then made a zigzag motion as she moved her hand away from her face.

"Lightning," Joe interpreted for Ryder's benefit.

Hannah nodded. "My grandmother said this girl came to her rescue like a bolt of lightning, saving her from the humiliation of having her hair cut off. This girl became like a sister to my grandmother. That must have been your grandmother, Ryder."

Ryder shrugged. "The one thing I remember most about my grandmother was that she cheated when she played cards with us and would sneak us forbidden lemon drops." He wanted to hear more about his uncle. "It's hard to believe Uncle Lance was a hell-raiser. He's a dignified judge in Washington, D.C. Evidently whatever happened to him here straightened him out."

"From what I heard," said Joe, "he lived in a hogan, tended sheep, and generally worked his butt off from sunup to sundown. According to the story my mother told me, a summer of hard work, discipline, and quiet talks with Dawn Skylark gave Lancelot Knight a new perspective on life in general and his own behavior in particular."

Hannah glanced at Ryder. "Lancelot?" she asked, unable to restrain a teasing smile.

"My ancestors had a thing about King Arthur and the Round Table," he admitted. "We all got stuck with Arthurian names."

"Every one?" she asked, leaning forward. "Did you?"

"Don't get Joe off the subject of how he came to work for my company. He's on a roll."

"Sorry," she murmured, and filed the question away for another time. She suspected he'd already answered it by his defensive attitude. She made a gesture toward Joe for him to continue.

Instead, Joe glanced at Ryder, then Hannah. "Are you two married or something?"

Ryder laughed.

Hannah frowned.

Their reactions didn't satisfy Joe. "Just what is going on between you two?"

"Nothing," Hannah answered.

"Everything," Ryder answered at the same time.

"Gee, that clears it up," Joe said.

"It's a little early for labels, Joe," Ryder said. "We'll get back to you when there's something definite to report. Why don't you finish telling us how you ended up in Houston at Wildcat Drilling?"

Joe waited until the waitress whisked by to refill their cups and plunk down more cream. "Apparently, Hannah's grandmother had stayed in touch with Mrs. Knight over the years. King came out to visit several times with his brother after Lance had gone on to college, and later King brought his wife and one or two of the kids. Probably your older brothers, Ryder."

"My grandmother didn't like to read or write English," Hannah said, still finding the connection difficult to believe. "She always asked me to do the books, the ordering, and all the correspondence at the store once I was old enough. I would have remembered writing to someone back east."

Joe shrugged. "She must have kept in touch with Mrs. Knight on her own. Does it matter?"

"I guess not," murmured Hannah, feeling hurt that her grandmother hadn't confided in her. Dawn Skylark's friendship with Ryder's grandmother was the second revelation she had had recently concerning her grandmother, the first being her having requested a survey of her land three years earlier. Hannah couldn't help wondering what other bits of the past were going to pop up.

"It gets even more odd," Joe went on, "considering your family and Ryder's hadn't seen each other for years when Dawn Skylark came to tell me about the job opening with Wildcat Drilling. Time and distance apparently hadn't diminished the friendship. That night Dawn Skylark said one of King's sons had started his own business in Texas and could use someone who was good with machinery. That was me. She managed to throw us together in a way that helped both of us."

Ryder leaned back in his chair. "My brother Michael once said he thought King would have made a great puppeteer because he likes to pull strings, especially ours."

"You don't seem at all upset," Hannah said, "that your father was interfering in your life."

"I have nothing to complain about. Joe was one of the best workers I ever had. Without his help keeping the first rig going, Wildcat Drilling might not have gotten off to such a good start. King did me a big favor. Knowing about our families' relationship also helps explain a couple of things."

"Like what?" Hannah asked. She was more confused than she'd been before Joe's explanation.

"I couldn't understand why your grandmother's file appeared on my desk three years after she wrote that she'd changed her mind about going ahead with the drilling."

"You didn't tell me she'd canceled."

"You would have slammed the door in my face even faster than you did if I'd told you that. Her cancellation notice was in the file. I came to Bacon Ridge because I was hoping to find out who was responsible for resurrecting the file, and why. Someone who knew me well enough to know I'd be curious about a phantom file made sure I saw it."

"For what purpose?"

Ryder's eyes gleamed with humor and an unidentifiable emotion. "If my father had simply instructed me to come here to Bacon Ridge, I would have put him off. This way it was my idea. He is a clever rogue."

"Your father wanted you to come here? Why?" As she asked the last question, the answer flashed into her mind like a neon sign. "Your father wanted you to meet me."

"Bingo."

Joe's head had been flicking back and forth between them as if he were an avid tennis fan at a championship match. "This trip to 'The Dating Game' has been fascinating, but I need to get going." Looking at Hannah, he said, "I haven't heard anything about your application being approved yet. I think the board is waiting for Pete Genay to make up his mind about taking a sabbatical so he can go wade around in the rain forest."

Hannah dragged her attention away from Ryder, who was still stunned by the revelations of the last few minutes. "Have they given Pete a deadline?"

"He has until May first."

"That will give me time to make up my own mind. The adult English classes are growing in attendance, and I don't have as far to drive as I would if I taught at Navajo Community College. A Navajo-speaking teacher is really needed here. I might decide I can contribute more if I continue teaching here."

"That long drive got old fast for me, which is why we moved." Joe made a face as though he'd bitten down on something unpleasant. "Did Nora tell you about her wanting me to build a hogan behind the house so our baby can be born the way our ancestors were?"

Hannah grinned. "I heard. Are you going to build one?"

"I suppose so," he grumbled. Turning to Ryder, he asked, "Remember those long nights manning the oil rigs when we used to talk about our plans for the future?"

Ryder nodded. "It sounds like yours worked out. I recall that you wanted to get a college degree, come back to teach on the reservation, find a nice girl, get married, and have four children."

"Yeah, well, I don't know about the four-kids part. Nora has three months to go before the first one is born. I don't know if I can take her getting odd ideas like building hogans each time she gets pregnant."

Hannah patted his arm. "Be brave. At least you don't have to do the hard part."

"You have obviously never built a hogan," Joe said.

"And you don't have to go through labor and childbirth."

He smiled sheepishly. "I see your point. I'll get to work on the hogan. Maybe I'll recruit some help from our mutual friend here, if he's going to stick around long."

Hannah shrugged. "You'll have to ask him."

Joe did, but he started his question with a long word Ryder didn't understand.

Ryder shrugged in answer. "I haven't decided how long I'll be here. You know, you've used that name for me before, but you'd never tell me what it meant." When Joe only shook his head and smiled, Ryder turned to Hannah. "Do you know what he's calling me?"

"I know what he said, but I don't understand why."

"Is it rude or embarrassing?"

"You'll have to decide that for yourself. He called you 'Man Who Makes Birds.'"

Joe chuckled. "I'd love to stay and hear your explanation, Ryder, but I'm going to catch hell as it is for being late, and I still have to pick up some material Nora ordered from the Trading Post."

Pushing her chair back, Hannah said, "I have some things to do at the store too. I'll go back with you and get Nora's order out of the store-room."

Ryder stood as well. "I'm sure Dayzie can find whatever it is Joe's wife ordered. We have some unfinished business to take care of before you return to the store."

"No, we don't."

"Yes," he said, a soft warning tone in his voice. "We do. You were the one who delayed it by running away. I won't be put off any longer."

FOUR

Joe's chair scraped on the linoleum floor as he got to his feet. "Are you two sure you aren't married? You sound like it."

He received dark looks from both of them. Chuckling, he took a step back. "Forget I said anything. If you can work us into your busy schedule, Ryder, I'd like you to meet Nora. Where are you staying?"

"Behind the gas station. In the Ark."

"That tiny trailer you used to live in? I would have thought it would be in the junk heap by now."

Ryder shook his head. "No, but if Bacon Ridge has a hotel I haven't seen, I'd be more than happy to take a room."

"Guess you're stuck with the Ark," Joe said.

"Looks like it."

Seeing they were ready to leave, the waitress swooped by to slap a bill for the coffee onto the table. Ryder reached out to grasp Hannah's hand while he tossed some money onto the table.

Joe's dark eyes gleamed with amusement as he stared pointedly at their joined hands. "I'll see you later then. Hannah can make the arrangements with Nora and show you where we live."

Ryder nodded. After they'd said their good-byes, Joe left the cafe. Ryder made no move to follow him. Instead, he walked over to the counter, drawing Hannah along with him. The waitress gave him a puzzled glance as she darted through a swinging door with a tray of dirty dishes. She was back before the door had finished swinging the other way.

"Will there be anything else?" she asked politely.

"Yeah." Ryder pointed to a pie that was on display under a clear plastic dome. "Is that an apple pie?"

Donna nodded as she shoved a pencil behind her ear. "Sure is. Baked this morning."

"I'd like to take it with me."

"One piece or two?" she asked, lifting the cover.

"Neither. I'd like the whole pie."

The waitress dropped the domed lid. "The whole pie?"

"The whole pie," Ryder said, smiling. "I'll take it with me." He took a ten-dollar bill from his shirt pocket and laid it on the counter. "This should cover it."

Donna looked at the money, at Hannah, and then at Ryder. "We've never had anyone buy a whole pie before. I'll check in the kitchen to see if I can find a box or something to wrap it with."

"Don't bother." He slid his hand underneath the pie tin. "I'll take it this way."

"Hey!" Donna called as he walked toward the door, taking the pie and Hannah along with him. "What about your change?"

"Keep it."

Ryder had to stop at the glass door, since both of his hands were occupied and he couldn't turn the knob. He looked down at Hannah. If he was reading her expression correctly, she wasn't in the mood to be cooperative.

"We can either stand here and wait for someone to enter or leave," he said lazily, "or you could open the door and save some time."

Reaching across him, she turned the knob and pushed the door open, but didn't make any move to walk out.

"Ladies first," he said.

Hannah hesitated a moment longer, but Ryder's purchase of a whole pie was intriguing enough for her to want to see what he planned to do with it. The few articles she'd read about King Knight had implied the artist was somewhat eccentric. Perhaps it ran in the family.

She smiled to herself as she walked beside Ryder along the sidewalk. They were drawing a number of amused stares from people passing them. She could visualize the phone lines humming like a barrelful of bees with this latest bit of news.

"You aren't angry," he said suddenly.

"No," she said. "I was thinking that I've had experiences with men trying to seduce me with flowers, candy, and moonlit walks along the beach in California, but I can honestly say a pie is a first."

"Whatever works," he murmured. "Did you leave anyone special behind when you came back here?"

"A couple of friends who lived in my apartment building and who used to have cheesecake feasts until the wee hours of the morning. We had a lot of laughs together, but the calories were hell on the hips."

"I meant men."

"I know you did."

She said nothing more, instead greeting several people she knew. She nearly laughed out loud when a man did a double take and ran into a streetlight pole. She didn't ask Ryder where he was taking her. Simple deduction led her to assume he was going to share the pie with her in his trailer, since the Trading Post was in the opposite direction.

When they approached the gas station, she waved to Billy Chee, who was standing at one of the gas pumps filling up the mayor's gas tank in his pickup truck. Billy raised a hand slowly in answer, his gaze shifting from her and Ryder's clasped hands, to the pie Ryder was holding like a waiter carrying a tray, then back to their joined hands. He was so intent on her and Ryder, he didn't notice that the gas nozzle had slipped from the car's tank opening and was dribbling gas on his new lizard-skin boots.

Ryder turned her toward the back of the station, where his trailer was parked. They had to walk around several oil drums, step over a couple of abandoned flat tires, and carefully avoid a haphazard pile of empty motor oil cans before they reached the cleared area behind the station. An orange heavy-duty extension cord snaked across the ground, connecting the trailer to an outlet on the outside of the station.

Curious about this place where Ryder had

been staying, Hannah studied the trailer. A variety of dents marred the aluminum sheets that covered the tiny home. The sun gleamed off the silver domed roof, and she imagined it could turn the trailer into an oven on wheels if the small air-conditioning unit on top wasn't switched on. Rectangles of metal covered the windows, keeping the heat out and the cool air in.

Having little experience with travel trailers, Hannah didn't even attempt to guess at its vintage. "Old bordering on ancient" would describe it nicely, she decided.

"Home, sweet home?" she asked.

"Something like that."

"Why do you call it the Ark?"

"On one of the job sites, I parked it in a spot that I found out later was called 'Washout Canyon.' Two raindrops could fall, and there'd be a gully-washer flooding the canyon. I slept through being washed about three miles away from the job site." He glanced affectionately at the trailer. "Damn thing floats." He lifted her hand, turned it palm up, and set the pie on it. "Hold this a minute. I'll be right back."

The fragrance of cinnamon and baked apples made Hannah's mouth water. As Ryder went inside the trailer, she broke off a piece of crust and popped it into her mouth. A juicy slice of apple was sticking out of one of the slits on the top crust. She removed it and greedily ate it too. Eating fried bread and rabbit stew with her uncle Atsidi for three days had given her an appetite for something sweet.

When she ran her tongue over her bottom lip to savor the spicy flavor of the pie, she was reminded of another hunger she was experiencing. A kiss had never lingered in her mind for such a long time, or made her think so much—too much—about the man who'd kissed her.

But then, it was the first time she'd ever tasted fire.

Her heart began beating a primitive rhythm as old as time when she thought of giving in to the desire that was growing in strength with every passing minute.

Even thinking about her mother's unhappy experience couldn't diminish her aching hunger.

Wanting a man she'd known only a short time was scary and exciting, though not very smart. It was bound to cause complications. Ryder was already showing signs of possessiveness, acting as though he had a right to know where she'd been the last three days. She wasn't used to accounting to anyone for where she went or what she did. She'd been on her own for a long time.

Inside the trailer, Ryder was thankful for the

air conditioner that kept the interior reasonably cool. He pulled out a drawer beside the sink containing a few basic kitchen utensils. Rummaging through the various knives, spatulas, and wooden spoons, he found one fork, then another.

He closed the drawer with his hip and wiped off the forks using a towel he'd moistened with water from the cooler. Luckily, the small chore didn't require a great deal of thought. As soon as he'd entered the trailer, he'd seen the note he'd jotted down that morning. He'd checked in with his office and his secretary had told him he'd received a faxed message from his father.

King wanted him to come to England next week. The summons itself wasn't so unusual, though the timing was strange, now that Ryder knew his father was behind this trip to Bacon Ridge. Even though he and his siblings had all gathered at Knight's Keep for King's seventieth birthday the previous month, rarely did a couple of days go by without King firing off a faxed message asking when they were going to come for a visit.

He'd also begun dropping hints about his children finding mates so they could provide him with grandchildren.

This message was different, though. King wanted to sell the gold Camelot chess set. The chess set had been handcrafted by an ancestor of theirs, and was nearly priceless. It was kept at Knight's Keep in a specially designed glass case, for which there were five keys in the shape of small shields. The case could not be opened unless all of the shields were in place. King had one shield, and each of his children had one. His message had instructed Ryder to bring his shield with him, as usual.

Like his brothers and his sister, Ryder had always taken the gold sculptured set for granted. It was a part of their heritage, a tradition to be brought out for a game or two whenever Ryder or the others came home. He couldn't think of a single reason King would have for selling the Camelot set. Money wasn't a problem. His father was an extremely successful equine artist, able to charge high fees for his work. Plus he still had controlling shares in Knight Enterprises, which owned a chain of upscale department stores with headquarters in Kentucky. Years ago, King had handed the controlling reins of Knight Enterprises to its CEO, John Lomax, giving the younger man the freedom and the trust to do whatever he wanted with the family business.

One of the forks slipped out of Ryder's fingers and clattered on the floor. He bent down to pick it up, his thoughts switching to the woman waiting outside.

His father's timing could have been better, he reflected. His intentions could have been clearer too. By tempting Ryder with the Skylark file, King had accomplished what he'd apparently wanted: Ryder had met Hannah. Ordering Ryder to travel to England so soon after meeting Hannah seemed counterproductive and a damned nuisance besides. Ryder was going to suggest to King that he stick to his painting and leave matchmaking to the experts.

He shoved the forks into his shirt pocket and rubbed the towel over a dinner knife before sliding it into his back pocket.

He had everything he'd come inside to get, but he didn't immediately head for the door. First he needed to admit that the reason he was sticking around hot, dusty Bacon Ridge had nothing to do with oil, his father, or Dawn Skylark's friendship with his grandmother. The reason was standing several feet away on the other side of the door.

Hannah was as much a mystery to him as the way she made him feel. He couldn't pin either one down to a logical equation, and he never would be able to if he didn't stick around.

He decided to stop wasting any more valuable time, since his days were numbered in Bacon

Ridge, thanks to his father's strange summons. He pushed the door open.

Hannah watched Ryder step down from the trailer. He'd left his hat in the trailer, and the hot Arizona sun beat down on his dark hair. Something tightened deep inside her as she watched him walk toward her. She had never met a man who could move so gracefully until Ryder Knight had strolled into the storeroom of the Trading Post.

He stopped only inches away from her, smiling as though he was aware of her thoughts. Leaning down, he brushed her lips with his in a gesture of casual intimacy that rocked her hardwon equilibrium.

He glanced at the apple pie and ran his tongue slowly over his bottom lip. "Couldn't wait?"

Watching his tongue glide across his lips, Hannah absently licked her own as though she could taste him. "Some temptations are harder to resist than others."

"Is that why you came here with me without too much of an argument? Because you were tempted?"

She wished she could tell what he was thinking. He was too good at concealing his emotions. Almost as good as she was—or thought she was.

She had to admit that he appeared to be able to read her quite easily.

"Yes," she answered honestly.

"By me or the pie?"

"At the moment, the pie is winning."

He grinned. "Do you want to go inside where it's cooler or eat the pie out here?"

"One temptation at a time. I'll stay out here. I would rather not give Billy Chee any more to gossip about than he already has. He's probably on the phone right now telling Dayzie to load up the shotgun because I'm being led astray by a wildcatter."

"What could be more innocent than eating all-American apple pie in broad daylight?" He again took her hand, this time drawing her with him around to the other side of the trailer. "When I lead you astray, I'll make sure Billy Chee isn't anywhere around."

"How comforting," she murmured.

On the back side of the trailer, a large tarpaulin was attached to the top edge of the roof. It stretched out about five feet and was held up by three aluminum poles that were pegged into the ground. A single lawn chair sat in the shade, along with a wooden crate that apparently served as a table. Another more solid box with a label advertising a popular motor oil had been placed in front of the chair where it could be used as a footstool. Ryder moved the second box next to the chair.

"Have a seat," he said, gesturing to the chair with a sweep of his hand.

She sat down, lowering the pie to her lap. Sitting on the box, Ryder took the dinner knife out of his back pocket and proceeded to cut the pie into wedge-shaped pieces.

"You didn't bring out any plates," she said.

He continued cutting the pie. "Plates have to be washed."

"Not if they're made of paper."

"I don't have any paper plates. You're lucky I found forks."

"How do you plan to eat the pie without plates?"

Whipping out a fork from his shirt pocket, he stuck it into the end of one of the wedges he'd just cut and lifted out a bite-sized portion. He held it close to her mouth.

"Open," he ordered.

Her lips parted.

"Bite."

Her eyes danced with silent laughter as she followed his instructions.

"Now chew."

She closed her eyes and made a soft purring sound deep in her throat. Ryder nearly came unglued. Buying the pie might not have been such a good idea after all. His original intention had been to use it as an icebreaker or a peace offering, whichever worked. Watching her eat the damn thing wasn't supposed to make him burn.

The pie was delicious, and Hannah wanted more. Since Ryder had dipped the fork back into the pie, she reached over to take the other fork from his pocket to help herself. Her lips were sticky from the sugary juices and bits of crust flakes dropped onto her skirt. Emily Post, Miss Manners, or her grandmother wouldn't have approved, but decadence wasn't always neat and tidy, she rationalized. This was one of those times.

She relaxed in the chair and happily finished off a slice of the pie.

She was stabbing for another bite when Ryder asked casually, "So how did you hurt your arm?"

FIVE

Hannah gave Ryder a cross look that was countered by a half smile. "No wonder Wildcat Drilling is so successful. You're so stubborn and persistent, I bet you'd drill halfway to China if necessary in order to find what you're looking for."

He didn't deny it. Nor did he let her change the subject. "Billy Chee told me you take off into the desert on your own quite a bit. No one seems to know where you go when you ride off into the sunset."

"The sun sets in the west," she said as she licked the tines of the fork. "I go east."

"It was just an expression." The sight of her pink tongue almost had him swallowing his. "Wherever you go is evidently dangerous, since you returned wearing a yard of gauze on your arm."

She had the feeling he was going to keep circling the subject of her bandaged wrist like a hawk hovering over an injured rabbit. To keep him from pouncing, she explained, "I take supplies to a member of my clan."

"You left out how you managed to acquire the bandage on your arm."

She shook her head slowly, feeling both irritation and admiration. "You don't give up, do you?"

"You might want to remember that," he cautioned. "You, on the other hand, are an expert at coasting around a subject without ever actually coming in for a landing."

"Since you'll probably keep going on and on about the bandage, I'll tell you what happened. It's no big deal. I burned my wrist. That's all."

Ryder waited ten full seconds. When no further revelation was forthcoming, he drawled, "Gee, Hannah. I don't know how to thank you for relieving my mind with such a detailed explanation."

She chuckled. "It was kind of flimsy, wasn't it?"

"Flimsy is something extraordinarily thin.

As a detailed account, yours was almost non-existent."

She looked around as if to make sure no one was listening, a movement Ryder copied without the vaguest notion of what he was searching for. Bringing her gaze back to his, she leaned forward and whispered, "You have to promise not to tell a soul what I'm about to say."

He crossed his heart and pointed to the sky. "I swear."

"I'm learning how to make Navajo jewelry."

Again, he waited. Again, nothing else followed. "I didn't realize," he said with exaggerated patience, "that making jewelry could be so hazardous. Explain that part."

"I accidentally burned my wrist on a piece of silver that I'd heated with an acetylene torch." She shrugged. "It isn't the first time, and it probably won't be the last."

Ryder was beginning to think the rumors he'd heard as a teenager were true: Unfulfilled sexual desire *could* make a guy go crazy.

"Let me see if I have this straight," he said carefully. "You go out into the flaming-hot desert for three days. Alone. To deliver groceries to a member of your clan and to make silver jewelry, even though the art of making jewelry is neither against the law nor a mortal sin, as far as I know.

Somewhere among the yucca plants and saguaro cactus, you have an acetylene torch that you use to burn yourself and occasionally some silver. How am I doing?"

"Sarcasm isn't necessary. You're the one who wanted to know what happened to my arm."

"I'm beginning to worry about you all over again, Hannah, if you think that puny couple of sentences was an explanation. Maybe you were out in the sun too long."

"You're making this much more complicated than it is."

"Me? All I'm doing is trying to find out how you got hurt. You're the one who came up with making Navajo jewelry on the sly."

"If people around here knew I was learning to make Navajo jewelry, they would want to know who was teaching me."

"That was going to be my next question."

"The man who is showing me how to work silver doesn't want anyone to know where he is."

A steam valve can only take so much hot air before it blows. Ryder's temper was approaching that point.

He stood abruptly, the top of his head nearly touching the canvas awning. "I was about to send out the National Guard to look for you, and you were with some other guy. That really frosts the cake, lady."

"Whatever that means," she muttered. "Stop pacing like an outraged wolf, Ryder. I wasn't with another man the way you mean. Atsidi is well over seventy, and my uncle."

Ryder stopped and stared down at her. "Your uncle?"

"My uncle. Atsidi was very well-known in the jewelry field about twenty years ago. His style of Navajo silver was unmatched. Still is, in many experts' opinion. Some of his earlier work sells for thousands of dollars. But he was badly exploited and made to look ridiculous at a jewelry exhibit. The sponsor who was arranging the exhibit asked him to make personal appearances in full Native American costume. And I mean *costume*. Even though Atsidi had his own ceremonial robes and headdress, he was asked to wear their version, which made tacky seem respectable, to put on their idea of war paint, and to pretend he couldn't speak English. He walked away, his pride in who he was much stronger than fame and money. Now he just wants to be left alone."

Ryder sat back down on the box. "Thank you, Hannah," he said quietly.

"For what?"

"For trusting me enough to tell me about your

uncle. I won't say a word about him to anyone. Not even King, who would probably trade his favorite paintbrush for the chance to meet your uncle."

"I wouldn't have told you if I thought you would tell anyone."

He leaned forward and touched her lower lip with one finger, then stuck his finger in his mouth. "You had a crumb on your lip."

The bottom seemed to drop out of her stomach, making her feel the same sensation she'd experienced once on a carnival ride. "It would make things so much easier if you would stop touching me every few minutes," she murmured, the pie forgotten. A hunger of a different kind was overriding any other craving.

"I like touching you. The only thing I can think of I'd like more would be if you put your hands on me."

"I barely know you." It was about the only thing stopping her.

"I think that's my line," he said with a rueful twist of his mouth. "You're a difficult person to get to know. You keep everything to yourself, where I like everything out in the open."

"Like the fact that you want to go to bed with me."

He didn't deny it. "The bed, the ground, the

table, standing up, lying down—I'm not that particular where." He smiled. "But I like to know who I'm making love with." Suddenly serious, he asked, "Who are you, Hannah?"

He was asking a question she'd only recently found the answer to herself. It had taken coming back to Arizona for her to finally find out.

"To understand who I am, you need to know where I came from. I don't mean geographically. I mean culturally."

"I'm listening."

She tilted her head to one side and studied him carefully to catch any sign of sarcasm. When she didn't find anything but his steady attentiveness, she continued, "I was raised mainly by my grandmother, even when my mother was alive. My grandmother was the one who took care of me, who answered my questions, scolded me, hugged me."

"What happened to your mother?"

"After she gave birth, my mother became very depressed. I was four when she rode off into the desert. Her horse came back; she didn't. She foolishly or purposely camped out in the dried-up streambed. A sudden rainstorm caused a flash flood, and she drowned."

"I'm sorry," he said quietly.

"So am I. I would like to have known her."

She set the pie onto the crate beside the chair. "I didn't speak English very well when I was sent away to boarding school, as most of the other children around here are. We lived too far from a school to go back and forth every day, especially since the roads were too rough for the buses to drive on. If you could imagine being suddenly dropped in the middle of a foreign country where the language, the food, the customs are all vastly different from anything you're accustomed to, it would be similar to my experience. Still, no one threatened to cut my hair and give me a bath in kerosene, so I suppose I was lucky compared to what my grandmother experienced."

Ryder's mind formed a picture of Hannah as a young child, frightened and alone, unable to communicate her feelings even if there had been anyone to listen.

He wanted her to know he understood the adjustments she'd had to make. "When my parents moved permanently to England, my sister and I were put into British schools. I was sixteen, Silver was fourteen. We'd always had Michael and Turner to run interference for us before, but they remained in the States to attend college. My mother was English, so I was familiar with a lot of the customs, the cultural differences. I didn't have a language problem, except for certain

English words that didn't mean the same as American words. But I remember feeling like a fish out of water, of being different."

She nodded. "I suppose every child hates feeling as though he or she is different. It's only when we're older that we understand it's our differences that make us unique."

"The way you were raised has made you the person you are today." He smiled wryly. "You had Dawn Skylark, and I had King Knight. Having him for a father is like living with Walt Disney, Rembrandt, and Charlie Brown."

"What about the fact that I'm half Native American and half Anglo?"

"I'm half American and half British. Does that make a difference to *you*?"

"Of course not," she said easily, then added, more seriously, "But there's also the fact that you'll only be in town a short time. I won't make my mother's mistake and get involved with someone who doesn't plan on sticking around."

He gave her a hard look. "I envy you."

Her eyes widened in surprise. She'd expected him to continue trying to persuade her to sleep with him. "Why in the world would you envy me?"

"I can't turn off wanting you as easily as you can switch your feelings on and off." He stood up and took a few steps away from her. Whirling around, he planted his fists on his hips and stared at her. "I don't like this gnawing hunger for you that's eating away at me. As irrational as it sounds, considering we barely know each other, I was worried about you when I couldn't find you the last three days, and no one seemed to know where you were. Getting involved with each other is probably the most scatterbrained risk either of us will ever take. I've tried not to want you. It didn't work. I think the reason you chose to leave to see your uncle was to get away from me. We both have a problem, Hannah, and we both know the solution."

Before she could respond, they were interrupted by an excited Billy Chee, who came running from the gas station yelling Hannah's name.

"I'm here, Billy." She sprang out of the chair. "What's wrong?"

Billy changed his course and met her as she stepped around the trailer. "You need to get to the Trading Post. Dayzie caught a shoplifter. She's holding him at gunpoint. I just called to tell her where you were."

Hannah had started running before Billy finished speaking. She raced past him, her pace quickening at the thought of Dayzie pointing her shotgun at a shoplifter.

She wasn't surprised when she realized Ryder was right beside her. By the time they arrived at the Trading Post, many people had gathered around the door. The Bacon Ridge grapevine had traveled at Mach speed.

Hannah pushed her way through the curious crowd and had to wade through even more people once she got inside. She shook her head when she was asked who had been caught, what had been taken, and had Dayzie shot the guy? She didn't know any of the answers, she told them, and she would never find them if they didn't get out of her way.

Since everyone was looking toward the store-room, she headed in that direction. Shoving aside the curtain when she finally reached the doorway, she expected to find even more people in her way. The only occupants, though, were Dayzie, still holding her shotgun, another clerk named Opal, and a twelve-year-old boy. He was standing against one of the support beams with his hands tied behind his back and around the post. A rope was wrapped around his waist several times.

Ryder pulled the curtain closed behind him, shutting out the people craning their necks to catch a glimpse of the thief, dead or alive. When he saw that the villain was a thin young boy who looked like the rope around him weighed more than he did, he relaxed and let Hannah handle the situation.

"Manuelito, are you all right?" she asked gently as she crossed the room to the boy.

He wouldn't raise his head to look at her. Nor did he answer. He kept looking down at the floor, his long black hair falling forward and partially hiding his face. His denim blue jeans were almost white from repeated washings and the material at both knees was split open and ragged. The white T-shirt he wore was clean but so thin it was almost transparent. His feet were bare.

Hannah turned to speak to Dayzie, and though Ryder was unable to understand what she was saying, he could tell from the tone of her voice that she was angry. Dayzie lowered the shotgun, and Hannah stepped around the beam to untie the rope. But all she accomplished was to break a fingernail, so she grabbed the knife she used to open boxes. When the boy's hands were free, he rubbed his wrists where the rope had chafed his skin, but he still didn't speak or look at her.

Hannah turned to the young woman who stood next to Dayzie. "Would you go into the store and tell everyone the excitement is over, please? And Opal," she added, catching the woman just before she left the storeroom. "No one else needs to know why Manny is here. Tell them it was just a misunderstanding."

Opal nodded and swept through the doorway. Ryder heard her raise her voice in an attempt to disperse the crowd inside the store.

Hannah stood beside the boy but didn't touch him. "Dayzie, tell me what happened," she said quietly.

The explanation was brief and in Athapascan. Since Dayzie also used expressive sign language, Ryder was able to piece together what had happened. The boy had taken some food, then had tried to run away when he was caught.

As she was finishing, Dayzie said something the boy obviously didn't like. Manuelito jerked his head up and glared at the older woman. "We do not take charity," he said in English.

"Thank you, Dayzie," Hannah said. "Why don't you help Opal in the store? I'll deal with Manny."

Dayzie glanced at Ryder, then said something else to Hannah in her own language.

Hannah shook her head and met Ryder's gaze. Ryder would have given one of his expensive new oil rigs to know what Dayzie had just said.

A few seconds later, Hannah satisfied his curiosity when she gave Dayzie an answer. She spoke in English, and he got the impression her reply was for his benefit as much as Dayzie's.

"I think we could use a man's point of view in this situation, Dayzie. I'm sure Mr. Knight will be more than willing to provide his opinion in this case, as he has so freely in others."

Ryder grinned.

Dayzie gave him a look that could have put frost on a cactus, then stomped out of the storeroom, taking the shotgun with her. Ryder stayed where he was. The boy was obviously desperate and scared, a possibly dangerous combination. He seemed harmless at the moment, but that could change. Ryder wasn't going to let Hannah and her soft heart be harmed.

Hannah leaned back against a stack of cardboard cartons, half sitting on the edge of one as she folded her arms across her chest. Manny continued to stare at the floor.

"Has your mother had the baby yet?" she asked casually.

His only response was a slow shake of his head.

"I'm going to make up a couple of cartons of food and some other supplies for you to take home." He jerked his head up, and she held up her hand to halt any protest he was about to make.

"This isn't charity, Manny. You're going to pay for every last can of food and bag of cornmeal."

Manny started to speak, but had to clear his throat first. He spoke roughly to hide the emotion in his voice. "I don't have any money to pay you."

"You don't need money. We're going to trade."

"I don't have nothin' to trade. He took it all."

Hannah didn't have to ask who *he* was. "He didn't take everything. Your father left the most valuable possessions here."

Manny frowned. "What?"

"You, and your brothers and sisters." She smiled at the blank look on his face. "We're going to make a deal, Manny. You're going back to school during the week. On Saturdays, you will come here to sweep floors and stock shelves. There's a bicycle out back you can use, once we put air in one of the tires, so you don't need to walk. When you go home on Saturdays, you will take food instead of pay."

"If I don't go to school, I would have more time to work to earn more food. I've been trying to get a job, but no one will hire me."

"Part of the deal, the most important part, is going to school. You're lucky you live only two miles from the school bus route, so you don't have to be boarded. You can come home every night to help your mother. No school, no deal."

The boy ran his fingers through his thick, coal-black hair, brushing it off his forehead. His shoulders weren't drooping with defeat and hopelessness quite as much as before.

"Is liking school part of the deal?" he asked, smiling slightly.

She smiled back. "You don't have to like sweeping floors either. Just do them both to the best of your ability."

"You aren't going to call the sheriff? Dayzie said I'd be arrested and that I would rot in jail until my teeth fell out."

"Colorful," murmured Hannah. "But not true."

Ryder concurred with the way Hannah had handled the situation, with one modification. "But Hannah will have to notify the sheriff if you steal again. That is, if Dayzie doesn't shoot you first."

Manny turned to him. "I won't take nothing ever again. I wouldn't have this time if someone had given me work. My brothers and sisters are hungry."

Hannah pushed away from the boxes and waved a hand in Ryder's direction as she walked over to a stack of empty cartons. "Manuelito

Chavez, this is Ryder Knight. Perhaps if I ask him nicely, Mr. Knight will help us carry the cartons of food out to my Jeep."

Ryder walked over to the boy and extended his right hand. Obviously surprised, Manny slowly lifted his hand, his movements unsure. Ryder waited. If the boy was taking on the duties of a man in taking care of his family, Ryder figured, he should be treated like one.

Hannah stopped sorting through the boxes to watch Manny respond to Ryder's gesture. It was probably the first time the boy had ever been treated as an equal by a man, she realized. His own father had never set much of an example, popping in and out of Manny's life at increasingly longer-spaced intervals.

Manny finally clasped Ryder's hand and pumped it several times, as though he were siphoning a bucket of water. Hannah was glad that Ryder neither corrected him nor laughed at him.

Ryder put his hand on Manny's shoulder to turn him around. "We'd better supervise Hannah's selection of boxes. She might pick out one that will hold more stuff than we can carry. We don't want to look like wimps in front of a girl."

Hannah turned back to the boxes, hiding her smile. Manny was actually swaggering as he walked beside Ryder! A few words from a man who didn't follow them up with a swat to the side of the head was having an amazing effect on the boy.

She ended up filling three large cartons with groceries, stuffing in a few paper products she had a feeling Manny's family was doing without. There was barely enough room in her Jeep for the bike, and Ryder suggested they leave it and make a second trip. But Manny looked so crestfallen, Ryder went back for the rope Dayzie had used on the boy and tied the bicycle on the back of the Jeep. When he untied it at the gas station so the tires could be filled with air, Manny insisted on doing the task himself. Ryder stood back and watched as the boy patiently applied the air hose to the tires.

After securing the bicycle once again, Ryder slid into the front seat beside Hannah and grinned when she murmured, "You're as tough as a marshmallow, Knight."

Hannah had to give Ryder credit. He didn't react with either disgust or pity to the abject poverty of Manny's home when they arrived at the hogan. Aside from a muscle in his jaw clenching when he first entered, he never let on what he was thinking.

The hogan consisted of one hexagonal room about fifteen feet across. The furnishings consisted of an iron-framed bed, a crib, two cots, an oil-drum stove, a picnic table, and piles of clothing. Blankets and other personal belongings were stacked against the log walls along with the clothes. The floor was bare dirt, hard-packed by years of being tramped on. Water had to be fetched from an accommodating rancher's well located a half mile away. Light was provided by kerosene lanterns.

Manny's mother, Lucy Chavez, was in an advanced state of pregnancy. Moving awkwardly, she greeted Hannah warmly.

"*Ya-ta-hey*," she said as she extended her hand.

Hannah introduced Ryder, and Lucy accepted him when she didn't see any sign of disapproval or distaste in his expression. When he asked if he could take the children with him to show him where he could fill the water containers, she gave her assent, after receiving a nod from Hannah that showed Lucy he could be trusted.

Hannah chatted casually as she helped Lucy put away the groceries. As she explained how Manny was going to work at the store, she made it sound as though the boy was doing her an immense favor, and never mentioned his attempt at shoplifting.

When Ryder returned, he followed Hannah's example and accepted Lucy's invitation to stay for dinner. If he hadn't personally packed the food they would be eating, he would have politely refused, even though that would have hurt Lucy's feelings. He would rather have bruised the woman's pride than take even one bite of food from the children and their pregnant mother.

Seated on the hard dirt floor, Hannah marveled at the easy way Ryder had accepted what had to be a cultural shock. Even if she hadn't known about his background, she would have figured he was accustomed to a more financially comfortable lifestyle than this primitive hogan in Arizona.

She smiled as he automatically grabbed Lucy's youngest toddler when the girl was about to lose her balance, tumbling the little girl onto his lap and proceeding to tickle her tummy. Then, to Hannah's amazement and the children's delight, he folded small sheets of notepaper to create origami birds and flowers, and gave one to each of them.

Now she knew what Joe had meant when he'd called Ryder "Man Who Makes Birds."

It was a ridiculous moment for Hannah to realize she had fallen in love with him.

SIX

Ryder raised his head at that moment, and Hannah looked away to prevent him from seeing the feelings reflected in her eyes. Just because she'd been stupid enough to fall in love with a wildcatter didn't mean she was ready for him to know it yet. Or that she ever would be. She needed some time to get used to the astonishing discovery herself, and then she'd decide.

Later, during the drive back to Bacon Ridge, they were both silent for the first mile, their thoughts on the family they'd left behind. The sun was setting over the mesas, the sky filling with shades of lilac, purple, and violet. The evening grew cooler as the sun lost its powerful strength.

Finally, Ryder said, "Now I know how Santa Claus feels after delivering a sackful of goodies to needy children."

"Except in this case Manny had to bargain away his free time. I wish there were other ways of salvaging their pride without making a boy trade his childhood for a man's responsibility of providing for his family."

"When we were packing up the boxes, I thought it was odd you weren't including anything from the freezers. You knew they didn't have any electricity."

"They live too far from town or any neighbors to have the luxury of electricity. It was an easy assumption to make."

"Will Manny keep his part of the bargain?"

"I hope so. He's the only chance they have."

"I counted four children other than Manny, and his mother is about to have another one. That's a heavy burden to put on the shoulders of a twelve-year-old kid."

"Many children grow up quickly here."

After another brief silence, Ryder asked, "Will Lucy have the baby out there by herself?"

Hannah didn't like the idea any better than he did. "Probably. It's doubtful she could ever get to a hospital in time."

"I could help a lot of boys like Manny by giving them jobs if you allowed my company to drill on your land."

"We've discussed this before," she said wearily. "I haven't changed my mind."

"You keep saying you don't want me digging up your grandmother's land, but she contacted Wildcat Drilling originally. After hearing Joe explain the connection between your family and mine, I think your grandmother trusted me. Maybe if I live long enough, you will too."

"Ryder, I really don't want to go over all this again. It isn't a question of not trusting you. Please don't think that."

"I haven't been able to think straight since I met you."

They drove on another mile before he spoke again. "I saw the blood on the floor of the storeroom where Manny was standing when he was tied to the post. That kid must have walked all the way to Bacon Ridge on that hot sandy road without shoes."

"His boots are probably saved to wear to school."

"I suppose he would refuse if I offered to buy him a pair."

"Probably." She paused, then said, "I've been thinking about how to come up with shoes for the whole family without making them feel they'd be accepting charity."

Somehow he wasn't surprised. "What did you come up with?"

"Lucy could make moccasins if she had some deerskin."

"And you're going to supply it?"

"If I can. I'll make a few phone calls and put the word out. After she has the baby, I'm going to approach her about making moccasins and other leather products to sell."

A few minutes later, Ryder said quietly, "You can't help everyone, Hannah. You're setting yourself up for a lot of heartache if you try. Some people you can help; some you can't. Some will want your help and others will resent it. That's just human nature."

She turned the Jeep into her lane. "When I first came back to this area, I learned I couldn't do everything, and that in some cases I shouldn't do anything. People can't eat pride, but that's all some of them have. It isn't my place to take it away from them."

"Why is it so important for you to help so many people? From what I've seen the last few days, the Trading Post gives credit to more customers than are paying cash."

"It's hard to explain."

"Try."

She was too tired to bother coming up with

anything but the truth. "When I was accepted for the teaching position in San Francisco, I thought I had everything I needed—a good job, friends, a terrific apartment. It was enough for a while. Then I realized something was missing, although I didn't know what it could be. I had everything I'd worked to have: my freedom, my independence, my own life."

She parked in front of the cabin instead of by the stable. Ryder was silent as she shut off the engine, then he turned toward her, laying his arm across the back of the seat.

"You haven't mentioned a man in your life," he said. "You're a normal, healthy woman. Did you stop to think that what you needed was a sexual relationship?"

"Leave it to a man to come up with that solution," she said dryly.

"We're such sexist pigs, aren't we?" he agreed easily. "In my defense, however, I'd like to point out that I have firsthand knowledge of how you go up in flames in my arms. My theory about sex being what you need isn't without some basis."

Hannah didn't argue with him. She *had* gone up in flames. And probably would again if he kissed her.

"You wanted me to explain why I try to help

people," she said. "When my grandmother became ill, I returned to Bacon Ridge to take care of her. That's when I discovered a major error in my thinking. My problem wasn't that I didn't have what I needed. It was that no one needed me until I came back here."

His fingers played with a strand of her hair. "What if I said *I* needed you? Right now? Tonight?"

She brought her hand up to remove his from her hair, but he turned this hand over and took possession of her fingers. "What you need any woman can provide, Ryder. I'm not into one-night stands."

"You might find this hard to believe, but I'm not interested in hit-and-run sex with you either."

To emphasize her point, she went on. "You saw the life Lucy has—the poverty, the hopelessness. There are a lot of Lucys in this world, my mother included, who pinned all their hopes and dreams on a man instead of relying on themselves. I don't plan to be one of them."

He brought their hands down to his hard thigh and ran his thumb over her palm while his fingers played with hers.

"Not all relationships end up like Lucy's or your mother's, Hannah. My parents were very close friends, as well as lovers and caring parents, up until the day my mother died. Joe Underhill and his wife seem to have a good marriage, so you know it is possible for a man and a woman to have a happy relationship. So, what are we going to do about this attraction between us?"

"Ignore it?"

Ryder shook his head and smiled when he felt her pulse increase under his thumb. "That's like trying to ignore a sandstorm when you're in the middle of it. You do so much for everyone else, why not do something for yourself?"

"Such as give in to my baser instincts and have a fling with a cowboy passing through town? That's not my style."

He flattened her hand so her palm was pressed against his thigh. "Hanging around a town just to be near a particular woman isn't my style, either, but that's what I've been doing lately. Maybe it's time for *both* of us to step out of character for once."

"I'll think about getting involved with you if you'll answer one question."

He wondered if she was aware she was sliding her fingers slowly over his denim-clad thigh. He'd never been more aware of anything in his life.

"What's the question?"

"What else are you looking for when you go from place to place, other than oil and mineral deposits?"

Her question knocked him off balance. "What makes you think I'm searching for anything besides oil and minerals?"

"You come from a wealthy background, so money for the sake of money wouldn't be your sole objective. It's usually people who've never had money who try to accumulate as much as they can. Since I've eliminated money, I'm curious about what drives a wildcatter to keep gambling on finding the pot of gold at the end of one rainbow after the other."

"A month ago, I might have had an answer for you. I'd have said I look for adventure, a challenge, the thrill of the chase."

"And now?"

He met her gaze directly. "For the last several months something's been missing. I thought my restlessness was caused by sitting behind a desk too long directing others out in the field. I hitched up the old trailer and took off with the idea of getting my hands dirty again. I guess I was hoping to find the excitement I once felt when I searched for the next big gusher or the next rich mineral deposit."

"Then you arrive in Bacon Ridge, and I

wouldn't let you check out my grandmother's land."

"Something like that." He lifted her hand and spread her palm and fingers out to match his. "I've made a discovery of another kind since I arrived," he murmured as he studied how small and delicate her hand was against his.

"And what's that?"

He looked up when he heard the breathless quality in her voice. His smile was slight, his gaze knowing. "I think you know the answer."

"Do I?"

"Sure you do." He enclosed her hand between both of his. "You know that some things are out of our control. Like this attraction or chemistry or whatever the hell you want to call it that's between us. It's time we do something about it."

"Gee, Mr. Knight. You certainly know how to sweep a girl off her feet with romantic gestures."

"If you're expecting me to whisper sweet nothings in your ear or shower you with flowers and boxes of candy, you're going to be very disappointed. It's not my style."

"I noticed that," she murmured. "Yours is more warm apple pie and making little paper birds. Which reminds me, I was going to ask where you learned to do origami."

"You're changing the subject. We were discussing having an affair."

"*You* were discussing an affair. I want to know how a wildcatter learns to make paper animals."

"A kid in my class in junior high occasionally ended up in detention at the same time I was there. I was fascinated with the different things he made out of paper to entertain himself, and he eventually showed me how to make a few simple things. Later, I found some books on the subject. Now that I've satisfied your curiosity, when are you going to agree to go to bed with me?"

"You don't suppose you could manage to be less blunt, could you? 'Your bed or mine, toots?' isn't exactly what a woman likes to hear."

"I wouldn't have any problems with you saying 'your bed or mine, buster.'"

She shook her head in a bemused fashion. "This is the most ridiculous conversation I've ever had. I have to give you credit for originality, though. You get your point across very clearly."

"I try," he drawled. "You promised to go to bed with me if I answered your question."

"I said I'd think about getting involved with you. There's a difference."

"Not a lot. Sleeping together is a damn sure way of becoming involved."

Hannah didn't know whether to throw herself into his arms or slug him. She felt like doing both, figuring either one might relieve the tension holding her good sense hostage. Her body was screaming for an end to the aching pressure of wanting him, while her mind warned her of the chance she'd be taking if she gave in to the demands their mutual attraction was making on her.

She sighed heavily, aware of Ryder's unrelenting gaze on her. "It would be so much easier," she said, "if you threw me over your shoulder and carried me into the cabin. Except I would probably fight you the whole way."

"Believe me, I've thought about it a time or two. The only thing stopping me is I need to know you'll be as crazy as I expect to be when I finally get inside you."

Hannah suddenly found it impossible to breathe. She knew her heart was still beating. Her blood was pulsing thickly through her veins, like molten lava. It was her lungs that seemed to have stopped functioning. And her mind, her practical, intelligent brain, didn't have a single coherent thought to work with.

But she could feel. Lord, did she feel.

Ryder heard the hitch in her breathing and

saw the stunned desire in her green eyes. He could have resisted if she'd said no. He couldn't resist when her body said yes.

"What the hell," he muttered as he reached for her. "I'm going nuts just talking about it."

His callused hands framed her face as he crushed her mouth beneath his. Her taste exploded on his tongue like his father's expensive Napoleon brandy, only more intoxicating.

Unable to get closer because of the gearshift between them, he broke away and cursed under his breath.

"If you want me to stop," he said roughly, "you're going to have to tell me how, Hannah. A few more seconds of touching you, kissing you, and the decision will be taken out of your hands."

She might have been able to refuse if she hadn't realized at Lucy's that she loved him. Her heart was so full of his magic, she needed to have him fill her aching body. She pushed aside a flash of fear. She wasn't her mother. And Ryder wasn't like the man who had fathered her. The situation between her and Ryder was very different.

As she met his gaze, though, she was unable to quell the feeling of apprehension that she was making a mistake she might never recover from. "If you stop now, I'm afraid my heart will quit beating," she said instead.

He groaned as he pulled her into his arms and buried his face in the curve of her neck. "I'm not sure what I would have done if you'd said no. The way you make me ache, I'd probably split in two."

She shifted closer to him, but was poked by the gearshift.

When he heard her mutter a distinct Spanish curse, Ryder chuckled. With his body as taut as a bow, he thought the last thing he'd be capable of was finding anything amusing. He lifted his head and looked at her. She made him happy, he realized. Just being with Hannah satisfied an inner craving he hadn't known was there. She made him feel complete and whole.

She placed her hands on his chest, sliding her palms and tormenting fingers over him. Even with his shirt between her hands and his skin, her tantalizing heat sent electrical charges throughout his system. He no longer felt like laughing.

He pushed his seat back as far as it would go and reached for the door latch. Once the door was open, he lifted Hannah over the gears and onto his lap. Allowing himself one more kiss, he took her mouth with all the hunger building up inside him. He almost lost what little control he had left when her thigh brushed against his hard arousal.

"I hope I can last until we're inside," he said through clenched teeth.

As badly as he wanted to taste her again, he forced himself to lift her up against his chest and step out of the Jeep. He didn't hear his boots crunching on the sand or see the sun drop below the horizon. All of his senses were centered on the woman in his arms.

Her front door was unlocked, saving them precious seconds. Once inside, he kicked the door shut behind them.

"Which room is yours?"

"First door on the left," she whispered.

The door was partially open, and he leaned a shoulder against it to push it the rest of the way. His boots rang loudly on the bare wood floor until he stepped on the red and black Navajo rug beside the bed. Still, he was oblivious to anything except Hannah.

Sitting her on the edge of her bed, he knelt down to pull off her boots. When the second one hit the floor with a thud, he parted her thighs with his hands to allow himself to move between them.

"What about your boots?" she asked as he started to unbutton her blouse.

A corner of his mouth lifted in a self-deprecating smile. "I'll be lucky to get my pants off." He parted her blouse and let his breath out slowly. "Lord, but you're beautiful, Hannah."

Needing to touch him as intimately as he was

caressing her, she fumbled with the snaps on his shirt. Her fingers were shaking so much, she gave up and gathered the material in her fists and pulled.

Ryder felt his head reel with the knowledge that she wanted him almost as desperately as he hungered for her. With one swift movement, he stood up and pushed her back onto the bed, then covered her with his body as he kissed her.

The world as they'd known it spun away as they created one of their own. Hunger caused groans of pleasure. Need created greed for more and more as naked flesh was stroked and caressed and aroused.

Ryder thought he'd experienced every nuance of desire that existed, but Hannah showed him how wrong he was. Taking, plundering, and giving, he whispered her name as he reveled in her. She responded to him with a natural sensuality that undermined his control and added to his pleasure. As the last of their clothing was swept away, he said her name again, this time as a question.

Hannah was astonished at how difficult it was for her to open her eyes and look at him. His long, hard body was pressing her into the mattress, his mouth only a breath away from hers.

When she saw the question in his eyes, she

breathed, "Don't wait any longer, Ryder. Please. I feel like I'm going to splinter into a million pieces."

"I know," he said hoarsely. He paused as he positioned himself, his muscles trembling with the effort of holding back. Looking deeply into her eyes, he warned, "Nothing will ever be the same again, Hannah. You know that, don't you?"

"I know," she said, then pleaded, "Ryder, please."

She lifted her hips in silent invitation, and he brought them together with a long, deep thrust. Her sigh of agonizing pleasure was echoed by his low, jagged groan.

He took complete possession of her, and she freely gave her heart and body. Ryder in turn was able to give of himself in a way that set him free, yet tied him to her with invisible chains of physical ecstasy.

Her fingers clenched and stroked as he took her higher and higher into an unknown realm of passion. Hannah cried out his name, and from what seemed a great distance, she heard him murmur hers as hot lightning flashed between them.

His hands slid under her bottom, lifting and holding her as he surged heavily into her. She clung to him as she was engulfed in a wave of completion that threatened to pull her under, but then flung her onto a high crest of pleasure. Ryder shuddered violently and joined her.

SEVEN

For the first time in years, Hannah didn't have the faintest idea what she was doing from one minute to the next. And for the first time in all those years, she didn't care.

When she'd gone away to college, she'd had a carefully laid out curriculum with a career goal in mind. As a teacher with a class of her own, she had worked hard to gain the sort of experience that she could use to help her people if she ever returned to Bacon Ridge.

Because of her grandmother's illness and then death, she had come back and decided to stay, but it hadn't been difficult to institute a new series of goals.

Now, with Ryder suddenly in her life, Hannah was taking life a day at a time rather than carefully arranging each minute and hour. She soaked up as many memories as she could for the future, when they'd be all she'd have. She didn't fool herself into thinking of Ryder in terms of a long-term commitment. He'd never once mentioned "love" or "forever," and she didn't expect either word. Fate had brought him there. She would wait to see what else fate had in store for them, instead of trying to control it.

If a tiny flame of hope stubbornly burned for a permanent relationship, she would just have to deal with it.

For the next two days after they became lovers, Ryder would pop in and out of the Trading Post, helping unpack deliveries and bringing lunch from the cafe for the clerks and Hannah. Each evening, he would arrive at her cabin and they'd prepare a meal, tend the horses, and spend the night together. Their lovemaking was still too new, too blatantly sensual, to take for granted. Instead of diminishing, it grew more urgent as desire became need.

Both evenings ended in the same way, with Ryder teasing, tempting, and tantalizing her until neither of them could stand the torture of being apart a moment longer. Ryder had absolutely no inhibitions or restrictions. Making love in the shower or on top of the washing machine was as natural for him as sweeping her off to her bed-room.

A few other things Hannah learned about Ryder during that time was that he had a fondness for chili peppers that could sear away the stomach lining of a normal man, and a natural sense of neatness that came very close to being irritating. Hannah was organized most of the time, but Ryder carried being tidy to new heights, or depths.

On Friday evening, she was standing in front of the sink washing a tomato prior to slicing it for a salad. She reached for the knife she'd laid down by the sink a minute earlier, but it wasn't there. She looked around in case she had set it down somewhere else, but she didn't see it. Puzzled, she opened the drawer where she kept the knife, and there it was, washed and dried, and in its proper place.

How could he have put it away? she asked herself. He wasn't even in the room.

"Ryder!" she yelled in frustration.

She heard the sound of boots coming from the bathroom, where he'd gone to wash up after helping her with the horses. A few seconds later, he was standing in the doorway of the kitchen drying his hands on a towel. His cotton shirt was unbuttoned, and his jeans were low on his hips.

"What's wrong?" he asked. "Did you cut yourself?"

"That would be very difficult to do, since you put the knife away before I could use it. You're going to have to do something about that nasty tidiness of yours."

"I thought women hated it when men were slobs," he said as he leaned a shoulder against the frame of the door. "What's wrong with putting things back where they're supposed to be?"

"Nothing, usually," she said dryly. "Except that I wasn't finished with the knife when I set it down on the counter. You slipped it back into the drawer when I wasn't looking."

He grinned and approached her. Looping the towel around her neck, he held on to both ends. "Is this your way of saying I'm infringing on your territory?"

"Not at all. It's my way of asking you to try to control your urges to straighten up. At least wait until I'm finished with something before you shove it away somewhere."

"I'll work on it." He pulled gently but relentlessly on the ends of the towel until she was pressed so closely against him, she could feel the hard planes of his body. "What about my other urges?" he asked softly. "Do you have any complaints about them?"

"I'm not complaining about your neatness fetish," she argued. "I'm merely suggesting you rein it in to a minor compulsion."

"Whatever you say," he murmured, bending his head so he could taste the sensitive skin behind her ear. He smiled as she slipped her arm around his waist without hesitation and leaned into him. "Even if I didn't burn for you as automatically as breathing, I would still go up in flames when you respond so naturally to my touch. I wonder if you have any idea what it does to a man to know he's wanted by the woman he desires."

A button on his cotton shirt suddenly became extremely interesting to Hannah. "I have caught a hint or two of your reaction during the last couple of nights."

"What's really bothering you, Hannah?" He released his hold on the towel and placed two fingers under her chin in a silent request for her to look at him. "Getting cabin fever? It was your idea that we hide out here. I've left my truck near the trailer like you asked so Billy Chee and everyone else would think I was there and not here. I understand why you don't want the gossips to discuss us over their fried bread and red beans, but I don't think we're fooling too many people."

The town grapevine was only part of the reason she was trying to keep their intimate relationship private. Another part was that the fewer people who knew of her involvement with Ryder, the less curiosity she'd have to deal with after he left town.

Privacy in a small town was difficult to maintain. Hannah didn't like the idea of her personal life being the topic of the day, or of comparisons being made between her mother's situation and her own. There was no similarity at all.

"I don't adjust to change quickly," she explained with a touch of self-mockery. "I don't rearrange furniture or shift things around. I make lists and mark dates on a calendar, and I'm used to living alone. I guess I'm not as flexible as you are."

"Are you having any regrets about getting involved with me?"

She smiled faintly. "Not yet."

"But you're expecting to have them?"

"Not regrets exactly."

"What exactly?"

"Ryder," she began without having the vaguest idea what she was going to say or what he wanted to hear. When his hands clamped around her waist and he lifted her onto the counter, she said his name again, this time in protest. "What are you doing?"

"I'm setting you on the counter. What does it look like I'm doing?"

He urged her legs apart and stepped between them. She put her hands on top of his solid shoulders, but not to push him away. Arousal beat heavily in her veins, affecting her breathing and making her needy for more of his magic.

"If you want the truth," she said honestly, "you are driving me crazy." She slid her arms around his neck as she leaned her forehead on his shoulder. "What am I going to do about you?"

He stood motionless, as if he sensed something momentous was about to occur.

"What do you *want* to do about us?" he asked.

Live happily ever after, she thought automatically. She knew better than to say it out loud, though. He was a wildcatter who liked his freedom to roam, to accept new challenges, confront different problems. At the first hint of possessiveness, he would be gone. That day would come soon enough without her instigating his retreat.

Lifting her head, she eased her arms from around his neck. "Don't pay any attention to me. Apparently I'm not as sophisticated and modern as I thought. Maybe I need to go into the sweat lodge and burn away the ghosts of the past."

"Ah," he murmured as if he'd just filled in the

last grid of a difficult *New York Times* crossword puzzle.

She frowned at him, trying to concentrate on their conversation, although it was becoming difficult. His hands were stroking her thighs with the familiar intimacy of a lover.

She dug her fingers into his shoulders and ran her tongue over suddenly dry lips. "What does 'ah' mean?"

The shade of blue in his eyes changed, deepened, as his thumbs brushed over the denim covering the apex of her thighs. A writhing coil of desire almost made her take back the question.

"You think I'm going to duck out on you like your father did on your mother, like Lucy's husband did, and probably too many other examples to count," he murmured against her throat. "We're going to have to do something about your lack of trust in me."

Tilting her head back, she closed her eyes as she absorbed the delicious tremors created by his warm lips. "Time will do that."

He shook his head in mock censure. "For such a beautiful, intelligent woman, you have a naturally pessimistic mind, Hannah. Remind me after dinner to talk to you about that."

He moved closer, slipping his hand under her shirt to stroke her bare breasts. Desire thrummed through her with deep, dark vibrations. His male scent filled her lungs. She hooked her legs around his hips and suggested they put dinner on the back burner.

He groaned. "As much as I like the idea of seeing how well we would fit together with you on the counter and me . . ." His hands shook as he slid them out from under her shirt. "Damn, just talking about making love with you is unraveling me, but I was referring to changing your mind about being so sure I'm going to fade out of your life."

When he drew back to look at her instead of kissing her, she shook her head as if to clear away the cobwebs of sensations. "How do you plan on doing that?"

"I have to go to England to see my father next week. I want you to come with me."

"*What?*"

Ryder blinked at her loud exclamation. "Your hearing is quite good, Hannah, although mine might never be the same. You heard me."

"You want me to go to England with you?"

"See?" he said smugly. "I knew you'd heard every word I'd said. So what's your answer?"

"I didn't hear a question."

His fingers tightened at her waist, a sure sign

he was losing patience. "About going to England with me."

She stared at him as though he'd lost his mind, then had to wonder if she had misplaced her own when she heard herself turning him down.

"I can't take off halfway around the world just like that," she said, snapping her fingers.

"Sure you can. There's nothing to it. I'll take care of getting our plane reservations. All you have to do is pack a few essentials for a couple of days."

"Even if I could leave on such short notice, which I can't, there is one little problem: I don't have a passport."

He shrugged. "We'll take the time to stop in Phoenix and get you one."

He made it sound so easy, she thought. Somehow she had to show him why it was impossible.

"Ryder, I can't go to England with you. I have too many responsibilities. I can't just ignore them on a whim."

He dropped his hands to her thighs. "And I can?"

He spoke in a tone of voice she'd never heard before. She didn't like it. "Apparently." She pushed against his chest, then slid off the counter when he stepped back. "You've been in Bacon Ridge for over a week. Our little town is hardly the hottest tourist attraction in Arizona. The reason you came here in the first place was because of the mineral rights you wanted me to lease to you."

"Which you refused. I'm curious what you think my reasons are for sticking around, since you've turned down my business proposition." His eyes narrowed. "Do you think I'm taking you to bed because I have nothing else to do? Or perhaps you think I seduced you as part of a grand plan to persuade you to change your mind?"

Hannah almost said yes, because she half believed it was true. She knew she should just say no and end the conversation, which was quickly getting off the original subject.

Instead she told the truth. "I don't know."

For what seemed like hours, Ryder stared at her. His expression was unreadable, his eyes strangely blank.

"Maybe you're right," he said at last. "Going to England with a complete stranger wouldn't be very smart. And it's obvious you don't know me, even though you've slept with me."

"That's not fair, Ryder. You're taking my refusal personally."

"You're damn right I am. How else should I take it?"

"I can't just think of myself. There are a lot of

people who depend on me here. The Trading Post is the only food store within a twenty-mile radius. I have no one I can count on to check the orders before they go to the distributors to make sure we get everything we need on a daily basis. If certain merchandise doesn't arrive, a number of people will have to return to their homes without food. Some of my customers can only get to town once a week, sometimes only once a month. They depend on me."

"We'd only be gone a week, not a month, Hannah."

Thinking of Atsidi, she said stubbornly, "I'm needed here."

Ryder seemed to read her mind. "You can hike off into the hills for days to take jewelry lessons from an old man, but you won't spare a week to go to London with me. That sort of puts me a peg or two down on the scale of importance, doesn't it?"

"That's not fair."

"I don't feel like being fair. Are you afraid the store will shut down in a week without you supplementing its cash flow with your own money?"

Her mouth dropped open in astonishment. She snapped it shut and muttered, "How did you know that?"

"Hannah," he said with deliberate patience,

"we delivered a couple hundred dollars' worth of food to Manny's family the other day. They certainly couldn't pay for it. I've noticed that more than half of your customers put their purchases on long-standing accounts. Not once during the time I've been in the store has anyone come in to settle up their bill. The suppliers are getting paid somehow or they wouldn't keep shipping merchandise. My guess is you're using your own salary or even your savings to pay them."

She couldn't detect any criticism in either his words or his tone. What she did see in his eyes was the look of someone who had been hurt and was trying to cover it with anger. It seemed remarkable to her that in protecting her own feelings, she had inadvertently bruised his. In order to be hurt, she reasoned, Ryder would have to care. She hoped that was true, but she couldn't walk away from her obligations either. She'd promised.

Somehow she had to make him understand why it was important for her to help her neighbors, no matter how tempting the idea of running off with him might be.

She held out her hand toward him, not entirely sure he would take it. "Would you come with me? There's something I want to show you."

"Does it have anything to do with why you won't come with me, or are you trying to change the subject?"

"Same subject." When he didn't take her hand, she dropped it to her side. "Different approach."

She took the kerosene lantern from the counter. After giving it a little shake to determine if there was enough fuel in the reservoir, she opened the back door and left the cabin.

Ryder heard the sound of her boots on the sand outside. He counted three footsteps before he swore under his breath and followed her.

He was going to lose this argument, he realized. He could feel it in his bones. Hannah would show him something that would explain what she'd been trying to tell him. Her refusal would make perfect sense, and he would have to go to England alone. He would be leaving her behind—which was exactly what she'd expected him to do from the very beginning.

He'd have to find a way to make her believe he'd be back. If he couldn't have Hannah herself, he wanted to at least know he was taking her trust along with him.

Outside, he saw she was heading in the opposite direction from where he'd expected her to go. Instead of the stables, she was walking toward the hogan behind the house. As he approached the entrance, he saw she had left the door ajar. He stepped inside, ducking his head in order to clear the frame of the door.

Hannah had hung the lantern from a nail in one of the log beams that crisscrossed overhead, in support of the mud-packed roof. A wood stove with a chimney pipe rising straight to the ceiling stood in the center of the six-sided building. A wooden platform the size of a single bed stood against one of the sides, a thin mattress on it and a sheepskin neatly spread over it. Unlike the hogan where Lucy was raising her children, this one was sparsely furnished and definitely cleaner and tidier.

Hannah was standing in front of a primitive rectangular table that used thick planks for its surface and lengths of birch saplings for legs.

She turned as he stepped inside. "My grandmother refused to have her hogan torn down after the cabin was built. She said there were too many memories she didn't want destroyed. If she'd died here, she would have expected me to keep to tradition and burn the hogan to the ground."

"From the things you've told me about your grandmother, she seemed to have managed to coexist in both worlds, the modern one and the ancient one."

Hannah nodded. "She was old-fashioned about some things and surprisingly up-to-date about others. She didn't like to read or write in English, preferring our own language. Even though she never read a newspaper or watched television, she knew what was happening in the world. For someone who maintained little contact with life outside of Bacon Ridge, she was remarkably knowledgeable about new discoveries and inventions. She believed in the old ways, but she also knew she had to keep up with current customs and laws. She would listen to the radio station that has a Navajo announcer, so perhaps that was one of her sources. She felt Navajo traditions were to be remembered and somehow incorporated with the rules of the outside world."

Ryder looked down at the table. On it lay an old leather pouch decorated with tiny beadwork and with fringe along the bottom. Next to it was a plastic box with the universal Red Cross sign on the lid.

"Are these her things?"

"Some of them. Her most prized possessions were buried with her. My grandmother was a medicine woman. She took great pride in being able to help people. As you can see, she mixed the old with the new." Hannah fingered the leather thong ties of the pouch. "There's a tribal saying that a man can't get rich if he looks after his family right. My grandmother believed that. Everything she had, everything she worked for, were for our clan and our people, not just for herself alone."

"You're saying that along with the house and the land, your grandmother left you the legacy of caring for others."

"I'd like to think I do what I can for the people because I want to, not because I feel I have to, although I did promise my grandmother to do what I could."

He looked at her. "Are you trying to tell me you've taken your grandmother's place as a medicine woman?"

Amusement glittered in the depths of her eyes. "It's not like handing down the family business. I never had what you might term a 'calling' to become a medicine woman. Besides, I'm too young. To be a medicine woman, one has to be past the childbearing years."

His voice low, his gaze direct, he asked, "Why have you brought me in here, Hannah? I don't have a problem with you wanting to do what you can for the people who live around here. What I don't like is you giving up so much in order to help everyone else."

"All I give is money and a little time. People are more important than a big bank account."

"I'm not talking about money."

"You aren't? Then what am I sacrificing?"

"Us."

She turned and walked away, wrapping her arms across her front. As it did nightly in the desert, the temperature had dropped considerably. Ryder suspected, though, that her gesture had nothing to do with the cooling air.

"You're the one leaving, Ryder. Not me."

"You're not asking me to stay."

She looked at him. "Would you if I did?"

"I can't," he said impatiently. "I have to go to England and find out if my father has finally lost all of his marbles, or if they're just rattling around in his head as usual."

She gave him a quizzical look. "You think your father is crazy?"

He smiled, thinking of the energetic, white-haired man he'd last seen a month ago. "Journalists in England are fond of labeling King as eccentric. It fits. The last label he would ever wear would be one that said 'Mr. Average.'"

He went on to explain about the Camelot chess set and his father's plan to sell it. "My brother Michael is already there, but King has taken off on a sketching jaunt, and Michael hasn't been able to talk to him yet. Turner is due to arrive in a couple of days, and we're going to gang up on King and stop him from selling our heritage."

"I understand why you feel you need to go, Ryder. You have an obligation to your family, as I have to my people."

"So where does that leave us?"

She shrugged. "It leaves us taking care of our responsibilities. You'll go to England, and I'll stay here."

A muscle clenched in his jaw as he gritted his teeth. She sounded so damn casual about their separation, he thought with more than a little resentment.

"You don't think I'll be back, do you?"

She sighed as if weary. Walking toward the door, she took the lantern off the hook. "We've exhausted this subject, Ryder. There isn't anything left to say about it."

He didn't move. "I can still think of a number of things to say about our relationship and your lack of trust in it and me."

"We don't have a relationship, Ryder. We have a strong physical attraction that we're getting out of our systems. That's all."

"You make it sound as if we have a disease and making love is the cure. And you accuse *me* of being unromantic."

"Don't use that word," she said tightly.

He blinked. "Unromantic? Why not, if it's true?"

The lantern swung like a pendulum as she turned abruptly to stand directly in front of him.

"Not that word. The other one."

He searched through what he'd said and tried to figure out which word had irritated her. "Disease"? "Cure"? "Making love"?

He didn't realize he'd spoken aloud till Hannah flinched when he mumbled the last set of words.

"Would you prefer the phrase 'having sex' instead of 'making love'?" he asked sarcastically. "Apparently, that's what's been going on between us. Just a brief sexual romp between two consenting adults until the itch goes away. Is that it? You believe history is going to repeat itself, don't you? That I'll leave and you'll end up pregnant. But—"

She didn't let him finish. She walked away from him and stepped outside the hogan. He followed, calling her name, and was just in time to see her lift the glass globe of the lantern and blow out the flame.

"Hannah, what the hell do you think you're doing?"

He didn't receive an answer.

Ryder cursed himself for having stared into the light. It was going to take a few minutes for his eyes to adjust to the sudden blackness. He couldn't see a damn thing. He heard a sound as though something had scraped the ground near his feet, then nothing. He strained to hear Hannah's breathing. Something, anything, to indicate where she was.

"Hannah, don't do this. Talk to me."

Unable even to see his hands in front of his face, Ryder reached back to find the solid wall of the hogan. When he felt the curved shape of a log and ran his fingertips over dried mud, he turned around and took a step toward the building. The toe of his boot struck something, and he bent down to see what it was. He sucked air between his teeth when his fingers touched hot glass.

He'd found the lantern. Unfortunately, it wasn't going to do him any good since he didn't have any matches. Once when they were kids, he and Michael had made a fire using the sun and a magnifying glass. That particular bit of woodcraft wouldn't do him any good now, however, since the sun had gone down and he was fresh out of magnifying glasses. He didn't have much faith in rubbing two sticks together, either.

"Hannah? Dammit, where are you?"

Wherever she was, she wasn't answering him. He hadn't heard any footsteps, but he sensed she wasn't there. He glanced in the direction he thought the cabin might be. If she had gone inside, she hadn't lighted another lantern.

Feeling around for the wire handle, he picked up the lantern, then trailed the palm of his other hand over the wall of the hogan just inside the doorway. He didn't remember seeing any matches earlier, but he was going to look for some anyway.

Then, when he could navigate his way back to Hannah's cabin, he was going to have a few more things to say to her.

Ryder didn't find anything resembling a box of matches when he blindly searched the hogan. His shin found the sharp corner of the bed frame twice, and his left elbow knocked into one of the hard logs framing the hogan once. Swearing under his breath, he finally sat down on the bunk to prevent further bodily injury while he went over his options.

Leaving the hogan in the dark would be incredibly stupid and possibly fatal. If he walked in the wrong direction, he could end up wandering around in the desert. There may have been a full moon, but it was blocked by clouds. The night sky was as black as crude oil and as impossible to see through.

He was going to have to stay where he was until morning, whether he liked it or not. Leaning back against the wall, he let his hand fall to the cover spread over the thin mattress. The sheepskin offered warmth, but at a price. A gamy odor rose from the skin, making him wonder how long it had been since the sheep it originally belonged to had been using it.

It was going to be a long night.

EIGHT

Usually Hannah enjoyed watching night shift into day. She liked to think of it as a fresh start, with new opportunities, a clean slate, and possibilities to change things for the better. Her grandmother had believed a person was healthier if he or she began the day at dawn. Every morning for as long as Hannah could remember, the older woman would step outside, look up at Father Sky, and say, "Today I will live well."

This morning, as Hannah observed the first fingers of the rising sun pushing away the darkness, she felt a soothing sense of renewal. She tipped her head back and closed her eyes. "Today I will live well," she said aloud in her native language, as an affirmation of who she was and a hope for the day.

She was on her way to Atsidi's cabin, having

left her own home four hours earlier. After she'd stranded Ryder in the hogan, she had stomped around her house, her mood alternating between anger and sadness. She had ended up sitting in a chair by the living room window, staring out at the night. Eventually she had realized the clouds that had been covering the full moon had blown away, leaving the nighttime world well-lit. She could easily ride to Atsidi's, especially since her horse Juniper knew the way so well. So she'd packed a few supplies Atsidi could use and led Juniper out into the desert.

During the first couple of hours of the trip, she'd told herself she wasn't actually running away from her problems. She'd only briefly tucked them away while she put a little distance between Ryder and herself.

By the third hour on the trail, though, she'd realized she hadn't escaped from Ryder and the harsh things he'd said. They were etched in her mind and in her heart; she'd brought them with her.

As the fourth hour approached, she was finally able to admit that the reason Ryder's words had hurt so deeply was that he'd confirmed what she'd suspected about him—that he had been indulging in sex while she had been making love. Hearing him voice her suspicions had touched an overly sensitive nerve, and his words continued to chime through her like a haunting echo. She had a feeling they would forever.

She acknowledged that one positive thing had come out of her brief involvement with Ryder: She now understood how her mother had thrown aside everything she'd been taught in order to be with the man she loved. Hannah had basically done the same thing, except she had been treated much better by her lover than her mother had. But like her mother, she had let desire overpower any thought of later repercussions. She should be thankful Ryder had taken precautions from the very beginning. She had been so wrapped up in her passionate response to him that first time, she hadn't even considered the possibility of becoming pregnant until later.

In the early-morning hours, alone in the desert, Hannah made a discovery. She realized she had been ashamed of her mother's weakness, of her involvement with an Anglo who had hurt her badly, and Hannah wasn't very proud of herself. Under the present circumstances, she had no right to judge anyone else. She'd tossed away a few of her own rigid rules after meeting Ryder Knight.

Once she'd worked her way through her own anger and hurt, Hannah was able to see that

Ryder had been angry, too, and perhaps for the same reason. It was possible he hadn't liked the thought that she might be using him for sex any more than she'd liked the thought that he was using her.

The more she considered his reaction, the more she had to wonder if she had been wrong in assuming he had truly given her his opinion of their relationship.

It was possible he'd only confirmed what he thought was her own assessment of their situation.

She clasped the reins in one hand and raised the other to rub her tired eyes. Her little jaunt was supposed to help her untangle her confused mind. Instead, she was only making the situation more complicated. About all she'd accomplished by her dash into the desert was to lose a night's sleep. She should have stayed and had it out with Ryder instead of leaving like she had. Her grandmother had told her often enough to stand and fight for what she believed in.

Where was Ryder now? she wondered. He had probably walked back to his trailer. Perhaps he was hitching it up to his truck and preparing to leave town. She couldn't blame him if he did. He'd tried to talk to her, and she'd literally left him in the dark.

Juniper's ears flicked back and forth nervously, and he shook his head several times. Hannah reached forward to pet his neck.

"What's the matter, Juniper? Do we have company?"

She was neither surprised nor alarmed. All sorts of creatures explored the desert when the temperature was cooler. The animals that stayed out of the hot sun during the day came out to find food at night. This wouldn't be the first time she had encountered one of the four-legged occupants of the desert.

Instinct, however, told her something other than a desert animal was out there, and she pulled on the reins to halt Juniper. They were coming to a narrow canyon between two high cliffs of rock. Once through the ravine, she had only a short distance to go before she reached the place where Atsidi had built his winter hogan years ago.

She turned her head in several directions as she concentrated on the familiar desert voices, listening for a sound that shouldn't be there. She didn't have long to wait. The clink of a horse's shod hooves striking rock ricocheted off the walls of the mesa.

She swung down from her horse and collected the reins in her hand. Ducking under Juniper's head, she stepped in front and led him into a wide niche that was hidden by a large outcropping of rock. There was just enough room for her to turn Juniper around to face the trail. She didn't take her rifle out of the scabbard, but she stood close enough to reach for it in case it was needed.

When she had first accompanied her grandmother on trips to deliver supplies to Atsidi, Hannah had been aware of the precautions Dawn Skylark took in order to secure his privacy. Several times in the beginning, they had been followed by reporters, and once by a jewelry dealer. When the publicity about Atsidi's disappearance had died down, Hannah remembered, her grandmother had relaxed her guard. Hannah still took the precaution of setting out during the night, but more out of habit and for the comfort of traveling in cooler temperatures than because of any fear of being followed.

She heard the clank of a metal horseshoe hitting rock again, closer this time. It was followed by another softer sound, which she recognized as human footsteps. Then a horse whinnied and Juniper replied. So much for the element of surprise, she thought grimly.

"Hannah," a familiar voice called out, "if you've borrowed Dayzie's shotgun, I'd appreciate it if you'd put it down. I'm too damn tired to pick buckshot out of whatever part of my body you happen to hit."

"Ryder?"

His voice came from the other side of the large rock, about ten feet away. "Who else would be stupid enough to chase after a stubborn woman half the night? I'm glad my brothers aren't here to see this. I'd never hear the end of it."

She stepped out from behind the rock after dropping Juniper's reins; the horse would stay where he was until she picked them up again. She saw Strumpet first, which answered her question of how Ryder had found her. The mare was as familiar with the way to Atsidi's as Juniper was, having made the trip numerous times in the past. All Ryder had to do was stay in the saddle, and Strumpet would do the rest.

Ryder was leaning against the boulder, his hat pulled low, one leg bent at the knee so the sole of his boot could press against the rock. He looked large, lean, and lazy with the sheer wall of sandstone at his back. He still wore the faded jeans, denim shirt, and black leather vest he'd worn the day before. A fleece-lined denim jacket he'd left at her house the previous night was rolled and tied behind Strumpet's saddle. His right hand was tucked into a front pocket of his jeans; his left hand held the reins. The way his hat was tilted, Hannah couldn't see his eyes.

"You're not stupid, Ryder," she announced. "You're crazy. What if Strumpet hadn't known the way? Do you have any idea how dangerous the desert can be if you don't know what you're doing?"

A full minute went by after her angry tirade during which the only sound was Strumpet stomping a hoof several times.

Finally Ryder pushed back his hat and looked at her. "So you do care." His voice was husky and low. "I wasn't sure."

If he'd meant to soothe her temper, he hadn't succeeded. "Why do you think I went to bed with you? Because I liked your face? I take back what I said a minute ago. You *are* stupid. Dumb as that rock you seem to be attached to."

Her raised voice had disturbed Strumpet more than it appeared to have affected Ryder. He didn't move or react at all.

"You're upsetting my horse," she muttered as she stepped forward and yanked the reins from his hand. "I'm going to put her with Juniper."

The few minutes it took to lead Strumpet to the niche in the rocks where she'd left Juniper didn't do much to cool her anger. She remained with the horses for a few moments, burying her face in Strumpet's mane and feeling like an idiot. It was time, she told herself, for her to act like an adult instead of behaving like a child just because Ryder wasn't following the rules. Part of her was happy he'd come after her, while another part wished she'd been able to come up with some answers before she saw him again. Shoving her hands into the pockets of her blanket jacket, she walked back around the large boulder.

Ryder looked like he had barely blinked while she was gone, much less changed his position. She stopped in front of him.

"I was coming right back to town as soon as I dropped the supplies off at Atsidi's."

"How was I supposed to know that?" he asked quietly. "The last time you took off, you were gone three days. I don't have time to wait around for you to wander back to town."

He fixed her with a fierce look. "After you stranded me at the hogan, I sat around sulking for a while. Eventually I realized the moon had come up, because I could see the ground outside the open door. The moon provided me with plenty of light to get back to the cabin. But you were gone. Since your Jeep was still there, I guessed you'd gone off on horseback." He shook his head. "Saddling a horse mostly by feel in a dark stable is an unforgettable experience."

She sighed heavily. "I shouldn't have left at all."

"Damn right."

She glared at him. "You're making it awfully difficult for me to apologize, Ryder."

He pulled off his hat and combed his fingers roughly through his hair. "I don't want an apology, Hannah. I want to understand what's going on in that beautiful head of yours. I know it wasn't easy for you to set aside your fears and sleep with me. I assumed your desire was stronger than your apprehension. Evidently, I assumed too much. I want to know how you feel about me, and I'll tell you how I feel about you. We'll work everything out from there."

The tightness that had bound her chest in a vice since she'd left the cabin loosened when she saw his half smile.

"You make it sound so easy," she said wistfully.

He pushed away from the rock and closed the gap between them in two long strides. With a flick of his wrist, he sent his hat sailing back toward the rock. Cupping her face in his hands, he said seriously, "It will be one of the hardest things you've ever done, because you're used to keeping your feelings to yourself. But I'm tired of guessing and getting it wrong."

Beneath the weariness in his eyes and his somber expression, Hannah could see a lingering sadness and hurt that surprised her, then made her feel humble . . . and ashamed. She'd been so intent on protecting her own feelings, she hadn't considered his.

The protective barriers she'd kept firmly in place most of her life were falling away, and there wasn't anything she could do to build them up again. Lack of sleep was making her feel lightheaded. That could explain why she couldn't stop thinking that he might care for her a little. He had come looking for her, after all. Or maybe his sense of chivalry hadn't allowed him to make any other choice. She loved him for being who he was, and resented him for the same reason. A bastard or a bully would have been easier to deal with than a Knight.

She brought her hands up to cover his. "You scare me, Ryder."

Of all the things Ryder had imagined her saying, those words were not even close. "You're frightened of me? Why? Dammit, Hannah, I would never hurt you. If you don't know that by now, we're in more trouble than I thought."

"I'm not frightened of you the way you're thinking. You scare me because you've come to mean too much, too soon. Throughout this whole night I've had nothing to do but think, and I realized I'm afraid of losing control of my life, of handing my pride, my freedom, over to you and not being able to get them back. It's not that I don't trust you to treat them well. I'm just not sure I could do without them."

Ryder removed her hat so he could see her face in the early-morning light, especially her eyes. The rising sun made her skin glow.

"I don't remember asking you to give up anything for me. I certainly don't plan on taking your pride, your control of your life, or your freedom from you. I was thinking more along the lines of sharing each other." He cupped her face again. "I'm not your father, Hannah, and you are not your mother."

Her smile was rueful. "That's not entirely true. Like my mother, I became involved with a wildcatter passing through town." He stiffened, then relaxed when she added, "But you're nothing like the man who was responsible for getting my mother pregnant. I've known that from the first day I met you." She took a deep breath and went on. "You see, he raped my mother when she refused to follow him from job to job without benefit of marriage. Then he left her and never came back."

Ryder pulled her into his arms, then held her tightly. She hugged him back just as fiercely.

Gradually, he loosened his embrace enough to ease back and see her face. From the very beginning, he'd been humbled by the trust she'd often placed in him. Knowing her past now, he considered it a miracle she had let him become her lover.

"You don't have to protect yourself from me," he murmured. "I would never hurt you."

He lowered his head slowly, giving her the chance to turn away if she didn't want him to kiss her. The dawn light appeared to be lighting her soul as she met his gaze.

The claim he made on her mouth was like the first time, for a moment, and then it was like nothing that had gone before. It was a moment of discovery and recovery, of response to needs yet unnamed.

A wave of pleasure threatened to engulf them in a sea of passion as he deepened his assault on her mouth. His hands lingered, hers clenched and caressed, as wordless apologies for having caused pain were exchanged.

Hannah felt the ground sway under her feet and vaguely realized Ryder was moving backward, taking her with him until he came up against the sandstone rock. Leaning back, he parted his legs enough to allow her to slip between them. He unbuttoned her jacket and slipped his hands inside, sweeping his palms over her waist and hips. Her breath caught when he pressed her lower body into the cradle of his hips. His gaze went to her mouth, then her eyes.

"This doesn't happen often between a man and a woman, Hannah. It's more than sex. I've never felt anything like the way you make me feel. If there are words for it, I don't know what they are."

She did. She knew what caused the emotion that was tearing her heart apart at the thought of him leaving for England. Until he felt the same way, she couldn't tell him not to go, nor could she tell him how deep her feelings for him had grown.

So she couldn't have forever, she thought. At least she had now.

Leaning into him, she arched her back and shifted her hips across the hard evidence of his arousal.

Ryder made a raw sound deep in his throat as a spear of white-hot need pierced his control. With hands that trembled slightly, he unsnapped the fastener of her jeans and lowered the zipper. He watched her face as he slid his hands across her stomach, then down into the opening of her jeans. She cried out when his finger caressed her intimately, the sound echoing against the rock walls.

Ryder felt as though he would explode if he didn't have her. Now.

"Hannah," he murmured, his voice as tortured as his breathing.

"I know," she groaned. "I know. This won't change anything, but if you don't make love to me, I'll shrivel up and die."

Her husky plea nearly pushed him over the edge. Gently, reluctantly, he drew his fingers away from her honeyed heat.

"Lift your leg."

With the toe of his boot, he pried off both of Hannah's, his gaze holding hers. When the second boot hit the ground, he shoved her jeans and panties down her slender legs, then lifted her off her feet.

"Put your legs around me," he rasped as he opened his jeans and prepared himself.

She obeyed, too lost in the sweet agony of wanting him to ponder the unusual position he had chosen.

Braced against the rock, Ryder lifted her, then slowly lowered her onto him. His breath hitched in his throat as she closed around him, hot and silky. She was his whether she was ready to admit it or not, he thought before she raised and lowered herself and he was no longer capable of thinking coherently.

Hannah shivered, but not from the cool air. Desire warmed her, fired her blood, and sent flames of pleasure through her body as he clasped her bottom to guide her movements. He took her slowly, then devastatingly fast, then slow again until the sequence had her gasping his name.

From a great distance, she heard him groan her name in answer. And then the world splintered away into a million fragments.

Ryder fought the surging release, willing the extraordinary magic to go on and on, but powerful shudders of completion rocked through him.

It seemed to take forever for the world to right itself.

"I can't let you go, Hannah," he said at last. "I don't want us to end."

Unshed tears clogged her throat, making it difficult for her to speak. "What are we going to do?" she murmured as she buried her face in his neck.

It was a question she had never asked anyone before, not even her grandmother. Dawn Skylark would have expected her to find her own answer.

He didn't answer. He simply kissed her lips before separating from her. The rasp of his zipper seemed abnormally loud when he straightened his clothing.

"Let's get you dressed."

She submitted to being dressed as though she were a child, although the kiss he pressed into her bare stomach as he knelt in front of her was very adult.

When he had finished helping her slip on her boots, he stood up. "This isn't where we end, Hannah. This is where we make a new beginning. I have to have you in my life. After we visit your uncle, we'll work out how." He paused, then asked, "Or am I taking too much for granted?"

Feeling as though she were standing at the edge of a cliff, she shook her head. "I want to be with you. I just don't see how it's possible."

He kissed her again, then raised his head and smiled at her. "You have to have more faith in knights, sweetheart. We're capable of fighting dragons of all kinds in order to claim our maidens."

Hannah believed him. "My hero," she murmured.

"You bet," he said smugly. "Let's go visit Atsidi. It's time I met the family."

They walked around the boulder to fetch the horses. Handing Strumpet's reins to Ryder, she said, "Atsidi's camp is on the other side of this canyon. I have supplies to deliver to him and some herbal medicine for his rheumatism. The length of our stay will depend on his attitude toward you."

Ryder wasn't reassured that her uncle would welcome him with open arms, but he figured Hannah wouldn't have asked him to accompany her if she thought her uncle would greet him with the business end of a shotgun.

Of course, he reminded himself, she could be wrong.

NINE

Once through the canyon, Ryder saw a thin line of smoke rising from a hogan in the middle of a meadow. A little higher on the mountain, snow still remained in patches, though he guessed it would be melting soon. Hannah had led the way until then, but once they were within sight of Atsidi's camp she waited for him to come alongside her horse. She removed her coat and laid it across the saddle in front of her. Ryder's leg brushed hers as he reined in beside her.

"Is something wrong?"

She shook her head. "I thought I'd better warn you about a few things. Atsidi lives by the old rules and will think you're rude of you call him by his name. He won't use yours."

"What should I call him?"

"Uncle."

"He wouldn't think *that's* rude? I'm not related to him."

"He's not my uncle, either, not in the way you are familiar with. He's the oldest member of my clan, which would be like an extended family to you."

"Anything else I should know?"

"We'll see how he receives you. I've never brought anyone to meet him before."

For some reason, that made Ryder feel less tired than he had a minute earlier. In fact, it made him feel damn good. "How are you going to introduce me? You'd better not say I'm your uncle, sweetheart. There isn't an avuncular cell in my body where you're concerned."

She lightly kicked Juniper's flanks with her heels and started off again. "I'm working on it."

Ryder followed. He hoped the introduction would be in English so he could understand the terms she used to present him to Atsidi. As he wondered what she would say, he realized he would have the same problem if she had agreed to accompany him to England. He hadn't given any thought to the wording he would have used to introduce her to his father. "Lover" would be correct, but too blunt. "Friend" was a bland term for what existed between them. "Girlfriend" wouldn't be accurate either. Hannah was more than all three, yet they were all appropriate as far as they went.

Ryder almost fell off the horse when he realized exactly what position Hannah played in his life. She *was* his life. He couldn't imagine going back to Houston and continuing his previous lifestyle now that he'd met her.

He was in love with her!

As astonishing as that discovery was, he felt something loosen deep inside him, something that had been coiled too tightly until now. The tension he'd been under during the long night ride to find her eased completely as he finally admitted to himself how he felt about her.

His gaze rested on her straight back and the thick black braid hanging down the middle of it. Hannah Corbett was stubborn, proud, and dedicated to helping her people. And he loved her.

Rearranging their lives wasn't going to be easy. Hell, he thought, getting her to accept the permanence of their relationship might very well prove to be the biggest challenge of his life.

Grinning like an idiot, he thought about the uninhibited way she'd made love with him on the other side of the canyon. She'd wanted him with the same intensity he felt toward her. What had started as physical attraction had developed into so much more. She made him burn with need, but with her he also felt more complete, entirely whole, as a man and as a lover. He was amazed that he could accept the changes he knew she would be making in his life. The wildcatter was about to be tamed, and he was looking forward to it. He might have to back down about Hannah accompanying him to England, but he wasn't going to disappear from her life as she expected.

How they were going to manage to be together was still a mystery, but they would work it out somehow. He was sure of that.

She suddenly stopped her horse, her gaze on the ground in front of her.

What's the matter?" he asked.

Pulling on the left rein, she turned Juniper. "There's a trail of corn pollen on the ground. We can't cross it."

Riding beside her, Ryder asked, "Why not?"

"I told you Atsidi goes by the old ways. It's taboo to defy the protection the corn pollen represents." Her gaze remained on the ground. "He always leaves an opening. I just have to find it. He has a few elders visit him occasionally, so he would have to allow them a way through too."

Ryder glanced past her to the six-sided structure still some distance away. The only sign of life was a stream of smoke rising from the center hole in the hogan roof. The wooden door was closed.

"He doesn't exactly encourage visitors, does he?"

"The corn pollen is to ward off more than humans," she murmured. "During the last couple of years, he has spread the line farther and farther out from his camp."

Ryder strained to see the line she kept talking about, but without any success. It wasn't until she made a pleased sound and turned Juniper in the direction of Atsidi's camp that he finally saw the corn pollen. A line of a white and light yellow substance, similar to the fuzzy down of a chick, had been spread out in a trail, except for the area Hannah had ridden through. He carefully guided Strumpet through the gap after Hannah.

As they approached Atsidi's camp, Hannah yelled something, her voice echoing off the high cliff behind the hogan. She didn't wait for an answer and kept riding. About forty feet from the structure, she called again, in words incomprehensible to Ryder.

Twenty feet from the door, she halted Juniper, and Ryder stopped beside her. She made no move to dismount, nor did she shout anything else. She sat in the saddle, her gaze on the door. After several minutes of nothing happening, Ryder turned to look at her.

"Now what do we do?" he asked under his breath.

"We wait," she said quietly.

"Maybe he's not here."

"He's here."

"How do you know that?"

"The smoke."

Ten minutes later, Ryder was about to suggest they check to see if the elderly man was really inside, when the door opened and a man with slate-gray and white hair stepped outside. Ryder judged Atsidi to be about Hannah's height. He wore leather pants and a leather shirt with long sleeves and intricate beadwork decorating the chest. Leather moccasins that extended to just below his knees were trimmed in leather fringe. A white strip of cloth was wrapped around his forehead. His eyes were black, his expression wary as he closed the door behind him. His bronzed skin was weathered with a few wrinkles from the sun, wind, and age, and his chiseled nose gave his face a certain nobility.

Atsidi was an impressive man, and Ryder was impressed. And intimidated.

A wide silver-cuffed bracelet with turquoise stones was visible on Atsidi's right wrist as he raised his hand with his forefinger and middle finger pressed together and extended, his palm out.

Hannah returned the sign, moving her hand to include Ryder in the gesture. Atsidi said something sharply to her, and she nodded in reply.

After a delay of several minutes, during which the elderly man studied Ryder thoroughly, Atsidi nodded abruptly and made another gesture with his hand indicating they could dismount.

Hannah unstrapped the leather bags behind her saddle and hefted them over her shoulder before walking toward her uncle. Ryder stayed where he was. He heard Hannah say something to Atsidi as she lowered the saddlebags. Probably, Ryder guessed, she was telling Atsidi what she'd brought.

Atsidi nodded, but didn't take the saddlebags from her. The older man's gaze ran over her, and displeasure creased his face, as though he'd smelled something bad. He muttered something that made Hannah grin.

Looking back over her shoulder, she explained. "Uncle doesn't approve of my wearing jeans. He called me 'Girl Who Dresses Like Boy.'"

Ryder didn't agree, although he tactfully refrained from saying so. No matter how Hannah dressed, she would always look to him like the sensual woman she was.

Atsidi's gaze shifted to him, and he spoke in a low voice to Hannah. She seemed about to protest, but the old man held his hand up to silence her.

Ryder wondered what in hell was being said. He wasn't reassured when Hannah glanced apologetically in his direction, then entered Atsidi's hogan.

As the elderly man strolled toward him, Ryder tried to convince himself that Hannah's uncle only wanted to have a little chat. But it was probably too much to hope Hannah's uncle had gone to boarding school and spoke English. Ryder noticed, with some apprehension, that although the man had to be in his late seventies, or possibly his eighties, his chest and arms were still powerful looking, and he had the crisp stride of a man who knew where he was going and why. Ryder wondered if Atsidi was just going to throw him back on his horse and order him off his land.

The older man's dark gaze swept over Ryder with the thoroughness of a high-powered microscope. Stopping three feet away, Atsidi nodded once, which Ryder decided was the only acknowledgment he was going to get. Ryder moved his head sharply in the same manner, his gaze never leaving Atsidi's. Still, Ryder had to use every ounce of control to keep from shuffling his feet like a nervous schoolboy standing in front of a stern principal.

Finally Atsidi said, in English, "The daughter of my sister's child has said you are her man. Is this true?"

It took Ryder a few seconds to figure out that Atsidi was referring to Hannah. An additional four seconds were needed to tamp down his joy at hearing the way she had introduced him.

He finally replied, "Yes, it's true."

Atsidi nodded again and began to walk away from the hogan. "Come."

Without any idea of what Atsidi had in mind, Ryder fell into step beside him. He wished Hannah had gone into more detail of what he should expect from this meeting. If Atsidi was going to question him about his intentions toward the daughter of his sister's child, he could start anytime now, Ryder thought impatiently. He was tired from a sleepless night and the debilitating fear he'd felt when he thought he'd lost Hannah. Now he was strolling around the countryside hoping for acceptance from a man who disliked people enough to stay as far away from them as he could.

They were approaching the area where Hannah had stopped her horse rather than cross the line of corn pollen. As he reached that faint line, Ryder realized Atsidi was several steps behind him. He stopped and waited. He didn't know if the taboo boundary worked the same way going out as it did coming in, but he wasn't taking any chances.

Atsidi stopped beside him, gave Ryder a look that seemed to see through to his soul, then turned to retrace their path back to the hogan.

Apparently, Ryder mused, he had passed a test of some kind. By respecting Atsidi's ways, Ryder had respected the man. In return, Ryder had earned the respect of the elderly silversmith.

They had walked about five feet when Atsidi spoke, startling Ryder so much, he stumbled over a clump of dried grass.

"You respect our ways. This is good. Not all people do. You don't feel the need to fill each minute with talk. This, too, is good."

"I would have ridden over the pollen if Hannah hadn't warned me off. There are many of your customs and traditions I don't know, and I might offend you out of ignorance. It will not be intentional."

Atsidi nodded. "I will not take insult. The little one has much heart, which makes for a bigger target for naked baby with bow and arrow.

She needs someone to watch over her while she cares for the People. Are you that person?"

The "naked baby with bow and arrow" threw Ryder for a few seconds, until it occurred to him that Atsidi meant Cupid. The "little one" was obviously Hannah.

"I want to be that person," he said quietly. "I want forever with her. I'm not sure that's what she wants. There are a few problems in the way."

Atsidi touched the back of his hand with two fingers, stroking the skin. "This not as important as this." He placed his right hand over his heart.

"The heart isn't the problem," Ryder said. "Nor is the differences in our culture. Her life is here and mine is in Houston." He explained briefly about his company, how he'd made something from nothing, and how a large number of people relied on him to employ them.

Atsidi gave one of his abrupt nods. His only comment was, "The heart will find the way."

As they neared the hogan, Ryder saw Hannah standing in the doorway. She was patting something back and forth from one hand to the other, her gaze never leaving them. As they approached, she went back inside.

As Ryder entered the hogan, he felt as though he'd stepped back to another time, back when the

Navajo people had lived without interference from the white man.

Hannah was frying the white dough she'd been slapping around in a skillet that rested on a grill over an open fire in the center of the dwelling. The smoke drifted lazily upward to the hole in the roof. She had folded her braided hair into a short club at the base of her head and had tied a white cloth around it several times. He realized she had secured the braid to keep it from falling forward into the smoke and spitting grease. She seemed perfectly at ease cooking on the primitive fire, and he wondered at this new view of her.

Feeling the older man's gaze on him, he looked away.

Atsidi sat on the hard-packed dirt floor and gestured to Ryder to join him. They were on the west side of the hogan, opposite the front door. Later, Hannah would inform him this was the place of honor for a guest to sit. She served the fried bread, and then Atsidi began to talk.

As he listened, Ryder got the sense Atsidi was like a dam that had built up so much pressure, it had finally burst.

Atsidi described how he was passing on his knowledge of silversmithing to the "little one," and Ryder realized how lonely the man must be, even though his isolation was his own choice. If

Hannah didn't visit him, Ryder mused, he would not only be without the food she brought, but he would miss her company. In order to escape being exploited and humiliated, he had become a prisoner of his privacy. One of his few links to the outside world, to supplies, to companionship, was Hannah.

Ryder began to understand another reason for her commitment to the people in the area.

Did he have the right to take her away from the people who needed her? he wondered. He imagined that in some cases, she was the only person whom those in need trusted enough to allow to help. Whether her extraordinary kindness was because of her ties to her grandmother or for Hannah's own benefit, she was important to a number of people.

Lord knows, she was vital to him.

Atsidi was demonstrating how a pump drill worked, using a piece of silver he'd placed on top of a small anvil, when Ryder felt Hannah's gaze on him. He looked up.

Hannah smiled faintly when Ryder caught her staring at him. She remained on the south side of the hogan, stowing the food she'd brought. Atsidi had waved away the cough medicine she'd included, so she put it at the front of a wood slab shelf stuck in between two logs, where Atsidi would see it easily after she was gone. When she was done, she sat on the ground with her back against the wall of rough-hewn logs, listening to Atsidi give Ryder his brief lesson in silversmithing.

The visit had started in the usual fashion, she thought. Her uncle had been characteristically withdrawn at first, as though he resented her arrival and his dependency on her for supplies. Normally he would be silent as she prepared their food and they ate. Afterward, he would open up and talk. She would answer his questions about her life and listen to his stories and legends while he showed her how to make certain designs and shapes in silver.

Today, however, he had a new audience. She'd been pleasantly surprised when the two men had returned from their walk, if not bosom buddies, at least talking to each other. Her Navajo side was pleased Ryder had the approval of her clan elder. Her Anglo side told her it shouldn't matter one way or the other. Both sides were relieved that a battle between the two sides wasn't going to be necessary. She wasn't up to fighting a gnat at the moment.

The sleepless night and the emotional tug-of-war she'd fought with herself earlier had taken their toll. She draped her arms across her drawn-up knees and rested her forehead on them. Her eyes closed, and she let her breath out in a sigh as she relaxed. She usually rested at least a night before heading back. Making the return trip later that evening when it was cooler wasn't going to be much fun if she didn't close her eyes for a few minutes.

Just before she fell asleep, she heard Atsidi's deep chuckle, followed by several coughs.

"I told the little one she could not come into the hogan until she could do a feather design right. All day she sit under the big tree outside pounding on the silver as though it was her enemy. When she finally treat it like a friend, the feather appeared. She has hard head, that one."

The last words she heard were Ryder's. "But she has a soft heart that counteracts the hard head."

When she awoke several hours later, she was the only occupant of the hogan. The anvil, hammers, files, and other tools weren't in their usual place. As she straightened, she became aware of a distant sound of hammering that she recognized, having made the same short taps on the anvil herself.

She smiled. Atsidi was showing off. Ryder was going to have a souvenir of his visit. As much as

Atsidi professed to hate company, he had certainly taken to Ryder.

So had she, she admitted. And she was only going to have one more night with him. Then he would leave for England.

He said he'd be back, and she believed him. What she didn't know was how long she could take fleeting visits between his searches for the next big strike.

What she had to decide, and soon, was whether to allow the affair to drag on, with each farewell tearing her apart little by little, or to make a clean break now and save herself a great deal of pain.

The unusual sound of Atsidi's laughter made her get up and walk over to the door. The two men were sitting in the shade of a huge tree about twenty yards from the house.

Hannah walked toward them. Atsidi was facing her, the anvil on the ground in front of him. Ryder's back was to her as he watched Atsidi hit a strip of silver around the curved end of the anvil.

Joining the men, she said, "I've never once found working on silver very amusing, Uncle. What is so funny?"

The hammer was pointed toward Ryder. "This one. He tries to speak the Dineh language. He wraps his tongue around his teeth and what should be one thing turns into another."

Ryder looked up at her. "All I did was repeat a word he said when he named the file he was using."

"What did you say?"

Ryder repeated the word, and Hannah chuckled. "I see the problem. You just said 'a pig has udders.'"

He grinned. "That's not even close, is it?"

"Atsidi also calls it a 'file,' like you do. Maybe you should stick with English."

"Oh, well. At least if I see a pig with udders, I'll know what to call it," he said.

Atsidi grunted, and Ryder raised his hand for another fitting. The cuff bracelet fit perfectly. With another grunt, Atsidi slipped it off Ryder's wrist.

Hannah didn't wait for Atsidi to tell her what came next. She stepped over a fire pit in the ground in front of a square hollow log and started a fire.

Ryder was fascinated by the artistry involved in setting turquoise stones onto the bracelet and in the engraving the silversmith accomplished with what appeared to be so little effort. With Hannah operating a set of bellows, the fire became hot enough to melt a plug of silver to be fashioned into coils to hold the stones.

The sun had started its descent when the bracelet was finally completed to Atsidi's satisfaction. Ryder put it on his left wrist and admired the workmanship.

Atsidi merely grunted and gathered his tools while Hannah put out the fire.

Ryder realized Hannah was taking an exceptionally long time to scatter the coals. Now that he thought about it, she had been unusually quiet ever since she'd joined them after her nap. Aside from their brief conversation about pig udders, she hadn't said a word.

He would have to wait until later, after Atsidi went to sleep that night, to talk to her alone.

TEN

Ryder's plans to talk to Hannah that evening had to be scrapped.

They had just finished eating the delicious lamb stew Hannah had set over hot coals earlier that afternoon, when she slipped on her coat and asked Atsidi what he wanted her to bring next time she came.

Ryder was drowsy from lack of sleep and quite content to listen to Atsidi's stories and watch Hannah in the firelight. Except when he saw her getting ready to leave. A four-hour ride on horseback to Bacon Ridge at this time of night didn't appeal to him. The wind had picked up outside, but it was warm and cozy in the hogan. Besides, he had spent an hour splitting wood for the fire and had looked forward to burning every single log. Getting a good night's sleep after he talked to

Hannah was right at the top of his list of how he'd like to end the evening.

"What's the rush?" he asked her without moving from his position against the wall.

"I told you this morning that I was returning home after I brought the supplies," she said while gathering up the pieces of jewelry she had worked on earlier under Atsidi's supervision.

"That was before—" He stopped abruptly, remembering they weren't alone. "Before I caught up with you," he finished lamely.

She shoved the leather pouches of silver into a saddlebag. "Have you forgotten you have a plane to catch for England?"

"No," he murmured. "I haven't forgotten. I didn't realize you were so anxious to get rid of me."

Atsidi rose from the floor with the grace of a man half his age and made a gesture toward the door. "See to the horses, Anglo. While you put on the saddles, I will tell the little one what I wish her to bring next time."

Ryder was about to protest when Atsidi jerked his head toward the door. "Go. I have given you a gift of a bracelet. Now give me the gift of respect by doing as I say."

Ryder pushed himself up to a standing position. He glanced at Hannah, then obeyed Atsidi.

When the door closed behind Ryder, Hannah faced Atsidi. "I do not wish to argue with you, Uncle. I know what I'm doing."

"I know what you are doing also. You are pushing Anglo out the door before he is ready to say good-bye. And I don't mean from this place. Do you wish to be rid of this man like he says, little one, that you shove him away?"

Hannah turned and took several steps away before pivoting around. "Wasn't it you who said the best way to get an unpleasant chore done is to do it? Putting it off for another time will only be more difficult."

Atsidi's sharp gaze nearly cut her to the bone. "Are you so sure he will abandon you? He does not appear to want to leave you. Could it be you are bandaging a wound before the knife has cut you? I know about running away, little one. You must have something better to run to than what you run from."

Hannah was stunned by Atsidi's admission, and the resigned sadness in his voice made her wonder if he regretted having lived like a hermit for so many years. Their relationship had been a long-standing one, but she had never crossed the line that had been established from the beginning. She was respectful and polite, but never personal. Until now.

She wondered if she and her grandmother had made it too easy for Atsidi to hide away from the world, not just the Anglo world that had tried to take advantage of him, but his life among his own people. He had cut himself off from everything, existing rather than living. He had chosen to stand by his rigid terms instead of compromising. When he could have been sharing his knowledge of silversmithing and giving people the pleasure of owning his beautiful designs, he'd been licking his wounded pride.

"Uncle?" she began, the barrier of years and respect forcing her to choose her words carefully. She never got a chance to say them.

He held up his hand to halt her. "We are not talking about me. My mistakes have been made. You can learn from them and not make them yourself. Anglo is a good man with respect for our ways. He looks at you with his heart in his eyes. It is up to you whether you break his and your own or not."

She didn't try to hide her pain. "It might be too late."

"And it might not. Regret is a lonely companion, little one. Do not take it on as yours when you have a choice." He paused, then began to chant the "Navajo Beautyway."

"I will be happy forever, nothing will hinder me.

"*I walk with beauty before me, I walk with beauty behind me, I walk with beauty below me . . .*"

His voice trailed off before he completed the chant. It wasn't necessary to.

Hannah smiled. "I will remember your words, Uncle."

Ryder opened the door and said, "The horses are ready, Hannah."

She nodded. Outside, she took up the reins, but before she got in the saddle, she turned back to Atsidi, who stood several feet away.

"It might be several weeks before I can make it back here."

He nodded. Then he crossed his arms over his chest, his hands closed into fists as a sign of affection.

She returned the gesture, smiled, and mounted Juniper.

Ryder walked up to Atsidi. "I've enjoyed meeting you. Thank you for the bracelet. Would you mind if I came back with Hannah sometime?"

"You would be welcome."

Ryder grinned. "Maybe we could have more language lessons."

Atsidi glanced at Hannah and said something in Navajo, a faint smile curving the hard line of his mouth.

Hannah chuckled and met Ryder's puzzled gaze. "You now have a new name: Twisted Tongue."

Ryder laughed and made the sign Hannah and Atsidi had made that morning: two fingers held out as a gesture of friendship.

Atsidi grunted and returned the sign.

Ryder mounted Strumpet and, with a final wave, turned the horse toward the canyon.

He and Hannah had reached the boundary of pollen when they both stopped their horses and looked back at the solitary figure still standing in front of the hogan. While they watched, the elderly man turned and entered his home, shutting the door behind him.

Hannah was the first to resume the journey. Ryder followed. Meeting the reclusive silversmith had been an unexpected pleasure. It had also been a revelation to watch Hannah in her role of caretaker. He'd seen for himself that she was indeed needed. There were probably others like Atsidi who relied on her for supplies and, perhaps even more important, contact with the world outside their remote locations.

For all the difference Hannah made in Atsidi's life, Ryder realized she received as much as she gave. As with her grandmother, it was her nature to help people. To take that away from her, he knew, would be selfish and leave her with a hole in her life.

The sun was setting behind a tall mesa as they entered the canyon.

Ryder found it hard to believe it was only that morning that they'd stepped into the sunlight shining down on Atsidi's private sanctuary. Now they were going back into the shadowed canyon, back to the problems they'd left behind.

There had to be a way for them to be together. All he had to do was find it, rearrange things—move heaven and earth, if necessary.

After an hour on the trail, he was no closer to finding a solution. That was when it occurred to him that he was no longer alone in making decisions, especially the ones affecting them both. He touched his heels to Strumpet's sides and urged the mare to catch up with Hannah.

"If I fell off the horse," he said, "because I fell asleep in the saddle, would you stop or keep going?"

"It depends on whether I heard you fall," she said with a smile.

"Terrific," he mumbled. Looking around them, he commented, "Is it my imagination or are we going a different way?"

"We're going a different way."

"A shortcut? Please tell me it's a shortcut that takes a couple of hours off the trip."

"Even with the nap I had, I'm still tired. I can imagine how exhausted you are. We're detouring to a place where we can rest a couple of hours."

"How far away is it? Tell me in minutes, not miles."

"Can you stay in the saddle for another fifteen minutes?"

"I might just make it."

She smiled at him, and he was mesmerized by the glow in her eyes. He sucked in his breath as her expression changed, as though a curtain had lifted to allow him to see her feelings. His chest tightened as he recognized the emotion reflected in the depths of her eyes.

"Hannah," he whispered in awe.

Her smile broadened. "Wait until we get to the cabin."

To hell with waiting, he thought as he leaned over and plucked her out of her saddle. She made a startled sound as he pulled her across his thighs. He wished they were anywhere but on horseback, but he had to touch her, had to have her body communicate what he saw in her eyes. Taking Juniper's reins, he wrapped them around his saddle horn so the horse would follow along. Hannah started to protest, but he cut her off by covering her mouth with his.

He groaned when she wound one arm around

his neck and the other slid across his back under his vest. She was straining against him, trying to get closer to his strength and his warmth. Lord, he needed this woman. Physically, mentally, emotionally, in every way. And if he was reading the look in her eyes correctly, she felt the same way.

The sound of Strumpet blowing a gush of air through her nose made him remember where they were. He lifted his head and looked down at the woman in his arms, the woman who held his heart in her small hands.

The sky had turned into a Technicolor display of violet and gold, with a streak of fluorescent purple slashed across it. Her skin glowed with the reflected light, and he had never seen anything more beautiful in his life.

"Why didn't you tell me?" he asked quietly. "I had a right to know."

She gave him a cross look softened by a glint of humor in her eyes. "I was going to confess how I felt about you when we got to the cabin whether you wanted to hear it or not. As usual, you have to do things your way. I should be used to your pushy nature by now. You've stomped through every defense I've put up since the first day I met you."

"Say it," he ordered roughly, his voice husky with emotion.

"I love you."

"Ah, Hannah. I wasn't sure I would ever hear you say those words."

"You almost didn't," she admitted. "I wasn't going to tell you before you left for England, so you wouldn't feel any sense of obligation toward me."

"Obligation? I feel a lot of things for you, lady, but obligation isn't one of them."

He kissed her with a devastating hunger that took her breath and sent flames of desire licking along her veins. Raw emotion blended with demand. The familiar weakness soared through her, making her feel strong with need.

When he finally raised his head, Ryder spoke against her mouth. "This place we're going—it better not be far."

She blinked several times. Finally able to focus and look around at their surroundings, she said, "See that large rock at the bottom of the mesa? The cabin is on the other side."

"Damn," he growled. "It's so far away."

"Less than a quarter of a mile."

He nipped at her bottom lip, then stroked his tongue over it. "I hope I can last that long."

She loosened her arms around his neck and

leaned back. "There's just enough time for you to tell me whether we're going to have sex or make love."

He looked startled. Recovering, he murmured, "We've been making love from the very first time, Hannah. At least I have."

She continued to look at him, waiting to hear the words. "Tell me."

"I love you, Hannah Corbett. I can't imagine living my life without you beside me." He smiled slowly. "Or under me or on top."

She tightened her arms and brushed her mouth over his. "Say it again, Ryder."

The movement of her body brought her thigh in contact with his hard arousal, and he groaned. "You're driving me crazy, woman. If we were in a car, we'd be in a ditch." He kissed her mouth hungrily, thrusting his tongue inside her warm mouth.

As they neared the rock, he lifted his head. "I love you, Hannah. I need to show you how much."

Hannah was restless in his arms, as eager as he to end the aching torment with their splendid lovemaking.

"The horse has more than one speed," she said breathlessly.

Ryder's body tightened with fierce arousal.

No one had ever taken him as high as she did, no woman had ever met the depths of his passion as an equal, giving and taking with as much feeling. The knowledge that she was as hungry for him as he was for her burned in his bloodstream like molten lava.

He held her securely against him as he encouraged Strumpet to canter. The rocking movement of her thigh against the front of his jeans had him clenching his teeth, yet he couldn't bring himself to push her away from him.

He felt as though a lifetime had gone by before he finally sighted the cabin. A mile more and he would have taken her on the damn horse.

By some miracle, he had held on to the reins during the ride and managed to pull on them to stop Strumpet in front of the cabin. He unwound Juniper's reins from the saddle horn and dropped them to the ground.

When Hannah realized he wasn't going to let her dismount by herself, she tightened her arms around his neck. He lifted her high against his chest, and spun around as he slid his right leg over the saddle horn, then slipped to the ground, still holding her. She buried her face against his neck as his long strides ate up the ground to the cabin.

She shuddered as need overcame any thought

but Ryder. Nothing else existed but him and how he brought her alive with his magic touch.

Hearing him say her name with a touch of impatience, she raised her head.

"Pull the latch, honey," he said.

The simple action wasn't as easy as it should have been, but she finally managed.

Ryder finished the job of opening the door by kicking it. Unlike the hogan, the cabin had several small windows. They let in enough light for him to see a cot, covered with a Navajo blanket, against one wall.

The small part of his brain still capable of thinking was relieved that the place was relatively clean—although he would have taken her on the damn ground if he'd had to, so great was his need for her.

He took a deep breath to try to slow himself down as he lowered her to the cot. He felt her fingers trembling against his chest as she attempted to unbutton his shirt. His own hands shook as he tugged off her boots and stripped her jeans and panties down her legs.

When her hand slid across his rib cage to the snap of his jeans, he groaned and buried his mouth against her throat.

Somehow he got his shirt and hers unbuttoned, and then he crushed her bare breasts to his chest, nearly exploding with the riot of sensations the feeling created. He wasn't going to be able to take the time to remove all their clothes; he needed her too badly.

"I can't wait any longer, Hannah."

"Then love me," she murmured. "Now. Don't wait."

Pushing her onto her back, he adjusted his clothing and covered her with his body, nearly losing the tenuous hold on his control when he felt her legs part to make room for him.

He forced himself to enter her slowly, afraid of hurting her if he unleashed the torrent of need built up inside him. She made a soft sound of aching pleasure. When she raised her hips, he was lost in her magic.

Even after their pulses had returned to normal, Ryder didn't loosen his hold on her. To keep from crushing her, he rolled onto his back, bringing her with him.

As much as he hated to break the cocoon of intimacy surrounding them, he was running out of time.

Her skin was still moist from their lovemaking as he slid his hand along her spine.

"Hannah?"

"Hmmm."

"Don't go to sleep yet, sweetheart. We need to talk."

"What about?" she asked lazily, covering a yawn with her fingers. Obviously, sleeping seemed like a much better idea to her than talking.

"When we get back to Bacon Ridge, I have to leave for England."

She opened her eyes and met his gaze, then lifted her hand to erase the frown on his brow.

"I know you do. I understand why you have to go."

"Do you also understand that I'll be back as soon as I can? That I love you and want us to be together?"

"You go do what you have to do. I'm going to be here when you can make it back."

As much as Ryder was relieved to hear her agree so readily to his plans, he was concerned by the hint of resignation in her voice.

"What made you change your mind about us?" he asked. "About giving us a chance?"

"It was something Atsidi said about pushing you out the door before you were ready to go. He made me realize that's exactly what I was doing. I was so busy trying to bandage the wound before it was even inflicted, I was losing valuable time I could be spending with you. I was wasting too much time worrying about how I was going to cope while you were away, when I should have been enjoying what time we have together."

He brushed his lips over hers. "We both have some major adjustments to make. One of which I'd like to make clear before I leave."

"What's that?" Hannah asked, hoping he would tell her again that he loved her. She knew she was never going to tire of hearing those three words.

"I'm not prepared to offer you anything permanent right now, but I don't want to have to get rid of any competition when I return. You might think I don't have that right, since I haven't put a ring on your finger, but that's how I feel."

A dead weight landed on her chest as she heard him say aloud that he wasn't ready to make a commitment.

She picked out the one word that seemed out of place. "Competition?"

"Yeah," he drawled. "As in other men. You don't need to worry about me, either. You're the only woman I want to be with, and I'll be busy trying to get everything taken care of with my father so I can get back to you."

Hannah's jaw ached from trying to maintain

her expression. She lifted his arm from where it lay between her breasts and slid off the cot.

She bent down to pick up her jeans and panties. "I know you could use some rest before we continue the trip to Bacon Ridge," she said as she picked up her jeans and panties, "but I'd just as soon get back as soon as possible. We both have a lot to do."

Ryder flopped back on the cot. Even the thought of standing up wasn't a pleasant one. "I suppose you're right, although I'd rather stay here in bed with you." He rolled onto his side, propping himself up on an elbow. "Promise me we can come back here someday."

"Anything's possible," she murmured as she buttoned her shirt.

Ryder detected an odd note in her voice he didn't understand, but he was so full of her and what they'd shared, he put it down to the same disappointment he felt at having to leave. But, he told himself, the quicker he got to England, the sooner he'd be able to return to her.

Suddenly full of energy, he rose from the cot and straightened his clothes. His mind raced ahead to the things he needed to do. "I'll make faster time if I leave the Ark behind. Would you mind if I parked it on your property rather than leave it at the gas station?"

"I don't mind."

Ryder was in his element making plans and decisions, his exhaustion forgotten, so he missed the rueful expression on her face. She was still fastening the front of her blanket coat when he took her arm and drew her along with him out of the cabin. He cupped his hands for her to step in to mount Juniper. She had to grab for the saddle horn to keep her balance when he almost catapulted her over the back of the horse in his eagerness to get going.

Six days later, Hannah set the clipboard and its stack of inventory sheets onto the counter and rubbed her eyes. Counting bottles of aspirin on the shelf had her about ready to take a couple of tablets herself.

Carrying pharmaceuticals in the Trading Post had seemed like a good idea, but they were tedious to inventory. Of course, the chore would have been easier if she'd managed to get even one full night's sleep over the past week.

The problem with closing her eyes was that a vision of Ryder as he'd been the last time she saw him instantly appeared, his eyes glittering with energy and excitement, his smile confident and signaling an impatience to be gone. He'd parked the Ark alongside her stables, unhitched it, and kissed her hard and quick before jumping back into his truck. She'd stood where he'd left her in the lane for a long time, even after the dust had settled.

She hadn't seen or heard from him since.

"I will finish that if you want."

Hannah turned to see Dayzie standing near the counter. "I'm almost finished, but thanks."

"You have always worked hard, child, but lately you do too much. You hire us to do some of the work, then you try to do it all."

"I like to be busy, Dayzie. You know that."

"I know you sleep little since the Anglo leave. That's what I know."

"I have a lot on my mind right now," she answered defensively, and changed the subject. "I'm thinking of carrying a line of deerskin like the one I found for Lucy Chavez. Several women have said they would like to make new dresses for the next Squaw Dance. If we have the deerskin available here, they won't have to go to Gallup or Phoenix to find what they need. What do you think?"

"I think you change the subject. Is it true someone came to tow the Anglo's silver house on wheels away yesterday?"

Dayzie's voice grated against her nerves like a

dull file. The older woman's topic of conversation wasn't doing anything for her either.

"It's true. Someone from Wildcat Drilling slipped a note under my door informing me that Mr. Knight had instructed him to take the trailer to a job site near Phoenix."

"Billy Chee saw it pass the station yesterday. You haven't heard from the Anglo since he left?"

"Not a word." Hannah met the older woman's concerned gaze. "You haven't said 'I told you so' once, Dayzie. I appreciate that. I know you didn't like my getting involved with him."

Dayzie shrugged her substantial shoulders. "He's not so bad. There are worse than him. I find it strange that he would just disappear like that. I know you said he was going to England to see his father, but don't they have phones in England?"

Hannah picked up the clipboard. She had gone past the stage of making excuses for Ryder. "They are quite civilized. They have telephones, a postal service, and fax machines. There are all sorts of ways for someone to get a message to Bacon Ridge—if they had something to say."

With the perception of years and long association, the older woman said bluntly, "You are angry."

Hannah smiled thinly. "That was yesterday's reaction. Today I've settled for disappointed. Tomorrow, I'll work on resigned."

Suddenly there was an unusual racket outside. Sand pelted the side windows as though a sandstorm had suddenly blown in from the desert. Hannah looked out front. Whirls of dust and sand were swirling along the street, but not with the ferocity of the blast of sand at the side of the store.

As abruptly as it had started, the loud noise ended, and all that could be heard was a rhythmic whomping sound.

Hannah tossed the clipboard aside, not particularly concerned where it went. She'd finally realized what was making the sandstorm outside. A helicopter.

A crowd had gathered by the time she stepped outside. She immediately threw up her arm to shield her face from the dust clouds still swirling in the air, even though the blades of the helicopter were barely rotating. By the time the dust cleared enough for her to see the helicopter, the crowd had a number of theories as to who the damn fool was who would land a helicopter in Bacon Ridge, and why.

Hannah held her hand over her eyes as she stared at the shadowy figure climbing down from the small cockpit of the helicopter.

The damn fool was Ryder Knight.

As she watched from the porch of the Trading Post, the crowd pressed closer to Ryder. Billy Chee slapped him on the back twice, and Tory from the cafe was grinning broadly. Hannah's eyebrows rose when she saw a Navajo woman grab his arm and pull him forward. It was Dayzie.

She heard Ryder laugh as the momentum of the crowd urged him toward the Trading Post. When he was within a few feet, the people buzzing around him separated and made a path for him leading straight to the porch steps and Hannah.

He stopped at the bottom of the stairs, placed one booted foot on the first step, and looked up at her.

"Do you know the second thing I'm going to do now that I'm back?"

She had to clear her throat before she could speak. "What?"

"Rig up a citizen's-band radio, a phone, or a walkie-talkie at your cabin."

Hannah was vaguely aware of Dayzie brushing by her to rush into the store. "What's the first?" she asked, staring into Ryder's eyes.

He started up the stairs slowly. His gaze was

simmering with barely suppressed heat, his smile one of sensual promise.

"What do you think?"

She raised her hands palm up, then let them drop to her side. "I don't know what to think."

Behind her, Dayzie was scolding, pushing, and ordering people out of the store. Ryder grinned when the older woman said, "Ten minutes, maybe fifteen, you can go back in the store. Right now, you stay out."

Ryder stopped one step below Hannah. His eyes were level with hers.

"You heard Dayzie," he said. "We have ten minutes of privacy in the store. We'd better not waste them."

Hannah just kept staring at him, so Ryder scooped her up in his arms and carried her toward the entrance of the store. Dayzie held the door open for him, then shut it firmly once they were inside. She planted her feet in front of the door and stared at the people milling around with grins on their faces.

Inside, Ryder didn't wait until he put her down before kissing her.

"Lord, I missed you," he murmured against her throat after slaking his thirst on her mouth.

Hannah didn't know whether to be happy to see him, or miserable because she would have to go through another good-bye when he left again.

She was neither for a few minutes as they hugged and kissed. When Ryder set her back on her feet, he looked down into her confused eyes.

"Why do you look so surprised to see me?"

"Probably because I am."

"I told you I'd be back. If I could have reached you by phone, I would have told you when I was going to get here. Every time I called, the store was evidently closed, because the phone just rang and rang."

At least he had tried to call, she thought. That knowledge, however, did not calm her turbulent emotions. "Did you get everything straightened out with your father?" she asked.

"It was as I thought before I left. He had no intention of selling the Camelot set. He was playing matchmaker. He admitted it. The only reason he ordered me to England was—he hoped—to speed up our falling in love." His eyes narrowed as he searched her face. "What's wrong, Hannah? You don't seem very happy to see me."

"Of course I'm glad to see you. I'm just surprised, that's all."

He lifted her chin to hold her gaze to his when she started to look away.

"Dayzie was more thrilled to see me than you are. What's going on?"

"I'm sorry," she said. "I'm new at this. I don't know the proper, or should I say improper, procedure. I'll try to do better next time."

Ryder was suddenly aware of faces pressed against the windows, and he took her arm to guide her to the windowless storeroom. After yanking the curtain closed and flicking on the overhead light, he leaned back against several sacks of grain, his arms crossed over his chest.

"Talk to me, Hannah. I thought we'd settled everything except for the details before I left. What's happened to change your mind?"

She took two steps to the left, turned, and took two steps to the right. Repeating the pattern, she tried to explain.

"I thought I could accept this, Ryder. I really thought I could. I didn't like it, but you said this was all you were ready to offer me. It came down to saying good-bye a hundred times temporarily or once permanently. Those were the only choices you gave me. I thought I could accept a part-time affair whenever you breezed back into my life. The minute I saw you climb down from the helicopter, though, I knew it would kill me to have to say good-bye to you again and then wait until you came back before I could resume living."

"I don't want you to say good-bye. I want you to say yes."

She stopped pacing and faced him. "To what?"

He shoved his hand into his pocket and withdrew a purple velvet ring case.

"To marrying me." He opened the lid and took out a ring featuring a malachite stone with diamonds around it. "At the cabin, I didn't have this with me. That's what I meant about not being prepared to offer you anything permanent at that time."

"Oh," she breathed, her gaze on the delicate ring. Looking up at him, she asked hesitantly, "You want to marry me?"

"No," he said. "I am *going* to marry you." He pulled her into his arms. "I have Atsidi's approval."

He kissed her softly, then almost desperately, communicating silently how long the days and the nights had been without her.

Pulling back at last, he framed her face with his hands.

"I'm moving Wildcat Drilling to Phoenix. The helicopter will make it easy to commute. There won't be any more separations. We'll need a bigger house than your grandmother's, especially when our children come, but all that can be worked out later. Right now, just tell me one thing. Do you love me?"

"Yes," she whispered, her voice choked. Then she threw her arms around his neck. "Yes! Yes! I love you, and I'll marry you."

He took advantage of her enthusiasm by kissing her until they were both breathless. He was tempted to pull her down onto the floor and give in to his raging need to claim her warmth, but he managed to set her away and take her hand.

Slipping his ring on her finger, he said, "Come on. We're getting out of here."

She had no practically run to keep up with him as he walked through the store toward the front door.

"Where are we going?"

He stopped at the door. "There's a cabin about three hours from here by horseback that we didn't get to spend enough time in. That helicopter out there can get us there much more quickly. It's the one place I can think of where we won't be disturbed."

Her eyes glittered with excitement and glowed with love. "For how long?"

He grinned. "Forever. You've tamed the wildcat for life, honey."

He yanked open the door and, holding her hand securely in his, walked outside.

The crowd cheered and clapped, and Dayzie wiped a tear from the corner of one eye.

In her own language, she sang softly, *"I will be happy forever, nothing will hinder me. . . ."*

THE EDITOR'S CORNER

The bounty of six LOVESWEPTs coming your way next month is sure to put you in the right mood for the holiday season. Emotional and exciting, sensuous and scintillating, these tales of love and romance guarantee hours of unbeatable reading pleasure. So indulge yourself—there's no better way to start the celebration!

Leading our lineup is Charlotte Hughes with **KISSED BY A ROGUE**, LOVESWEPT #654—and a rogue is exactly what Cord Buford is. With a smile that promises wicked pleasures, he's used to getting what he wants, so when the beautiful new physician in town insists she won't go out with him, he takes it as a very personal challenge. He'll do anything to feel Billie Foster's soft hands on him, even dare her to give him a physical. Billie's struggle to resist Cord's dangerous temptations is useless, but when their investigation into a mystery at his family's textile mill erupts into steamy kisses under moonlit skies, she has to wonder if she's the one woman who can tame his wild heart. Charlotte's talent shines brightly in this delicious romance.

New author Debra Dixon makes an outstanding debut in LOVESWEPT with **TALL, DARK, AND LONESOME,** #655. Trail boss Zach Weston is definitely all of those things, as Niki Devlin soon discovers when she joins his vacation cattle drive. The columnist starts out interested only in getting a story, but from the moment Zach pulls her out of the mud and into his arms, she wants to scorch his iron control and play with the fire in his gray eyes. However, she believes the scandal that haunts her past can destroy his dreams of happily-ever-after—until Zach dares her to stop running and be lassoed by his love. Talented Debra combines emotional intensity and humor to make **TALL, DARK, AND LONESOME** a winner. You're sure to look forward to more from this New Face of 1993!

Do you remember Jenny Love-Townsend, the heroine's daughter in Peggy Webb's **TOUCHED BY ANGELS?** She returns in **A PRINCE FOR JENNY,** LOVESWEPT #656, but now she's all grown up, a fragile artist who finally meets the man of her dreams. Daniel Sullivan is everything she's ever wished for and the one thing she's sure she can't have. Daniel agrees that the spellbinding emotion between them can't last. He doesn't consider himself to be as noble, strong, and powerful as Jenny sketched him, and though he wants to taste her magic, his desire for this special woman can put her in danger. Peggy will have you crying and cheering as these two people find the courage to believe in the power of love.

What an apt title **FEVER** is for Joan J. Domning's new LOVESWEPT #657, for the temperature does nothing but rise when Alec Golightly and Bunny Fletcher meet. He's a corporate executive who wears a Hawaiian shirt and a pirate's grin—not at all what she expects when she goes to Portland to help bail out his company. Her plan is to get the job done, then quickly return to the fast track, but she suddenly finds herself wildly tempted to run into his arms and stay there. A family is one thing she's never had time for in her race to be the best, but with Alec tantalizing her with his long, slow kisses, she's ready to seize the happiness that has always eluded her. Joan delivers a sexy romance that burns white-hot with desire.

Please welcome Jackie Reeser and her very first novel, **THE LADY CASTS HER LURES**, LOVESWEPT #658. Jackie's a veteran journalist, and she has given her heroine, Pat Langston, the same occupation—and a vexing assignment: to accompany champion Brian Culler on the final round of a fishing contest. He's always found reporters annoying, but one look at Pat and he quickly welcomes the delectable distraction, baiting her with charm that could reel any woman in. The spirited single mom isn't interested in a lady's man who'd never settle down, though. But Brian knows all about being patient and pursues her with seductive humor, willing to wait for the prize of her passion. This delightful romance, told with plenty of verve and sensuality, will show you why we're so excited to be publishing Jackie in LOVESWEPT.

Diane Pershing rounds out the lineup in a very big way with **HEARTQUAKE**, LOVESWEPT #659. A golden-haired geologist, David Franklin prowls the earth in search of the secrets that make it tremble, but he's never felt a tremor as strong as the one that shakes his very soul when he meets Bella Stein. A distant relative, she's surprised by his arrival on her doorstep—and shocked by the restless longing he awakens in her. His wildfire caresses make the beautiful widow respond to him with shameless abandon. Then she discovers the pain he's hidden from everyone, and only her tenderness can heal him and show him that he's worthy of her gift of enduring love. . . . Diane's evocative writing makes this romance stand out.

Happy reading,

With warmest wishes,

Nita Taublib

Nita Taublib

Associate Publisher

P.S. Don't miss the spectacular women's novels Bantam has coming in December: **ADAM'S FALL** by Sandra Brown, a classic romance soon to be available in hardcover; **NOTORIOUS** by Patricia Potter, in which the rivalry and passion between two saloon owners becomes the rage of San Francisco; **PRINCESS OF THIEVES** by Katherine O'Neal, featuring a delightfully wicked con woman and a rugged, ruthless bounty hunter; and **CAPTURE THE NIGHT** by Geralyn Dawson, the latest Once Upon a Time romance with "Beauty and the Beast" at its heart. We'll be giving you a sneak peak at these terrific books in next month's LOVESWEPTs. And immediately following this page, look for a preview of the exciting women's fiction from Bantam *available now!*

Don't miss these exciting books by your favorite Bantam authors

On sale in October:
OUTLAW
by Susan Johnson

MOONLIGHT, MADNESS, & MAGIC
by Suzanne Forster, Charlotte Hughes, and Olivia Rupprecht

SATIN AND STEELE
by Fayrene Preston

And in hardcover from Doubleday
SOMETHING BORROWED, SOMETHING BLUE
by Jillian Karr

Susan Johnson

Nationally bestselling author of
SINFUL and **SILVER FLAME**

Outlaw

*Susan Johnson's most passionate and richly textured
romance yet, OUTLAW is the sizzling story of a fierce
Scottish border lord who abducts his sworn enemy, a
beautiful English woman—only to find himself a captive
of her love.*

"Come sit by me then." Elizabeth gently patted
the rough bark beside her as if coaxing a small child
to an unpleasant task.

He should leave, Johnnie thought. He shouldn't
have ridden after her, he shouldn't be panting like
a dog in heat for any woman . . . particularly for
this woman, the daughter of Harold Godfrey, his
lifelong enemy.

"Are you afraid of me?" She'd stopped running
now from her desire. It was an enormous leap of
faith, a rash and venturesome sensation for a woman who'd always viewed the world with caution.

"I'm not afraid of anything," Johnnie answered,
unhesitating confidence in his deep voice.

"I didn't think so," she replied. Dressed like a reiver in leather breeches, high boots, a shirt open at the throat, his hunting plaid the muted color of autumn foliage, he looked not only unafraid but menacing. The danger and attraction of scandalous sin, she thought—all dark arrogant masculinity. "My guardsmen will wait indefinitely," she said very, very quietly, thinking with an arrogance of her own, *There. That should move him.*

And when he took that first step, she smiled a tantalizing female smile, artless and instinctive.

"You please me," she said, gazing up at him as he slowly drew near.

"*You* drive me mad," Johnnie said, sitting down on the fallen tree, resting his arms on his knees and contemplating the dusty toes of his boots.

"And you don't like the feeling."

"I dislike it intensely," he retorted, chafing resentment plain in his voice.

He wouldn't look at her. "Would you rather I leave?"

His head swiveled toward her then, a cynical gleam in his blue eyes. "Of course not."

"Hmmm," Elizabeth murmured, pursing her lips, clasping her hands together and studying her yellow kidskin slippers. "This *is* awkward," she said after a moment, amusement in her voice. Sitting up straighter, she half turned to gaze at him. "I've never seduced a man before." A smile of unalloyed innocence curved her mouth. "Could you help me? If you don't mind, my lord," she demurely added.

A grin slowly creased his tanned cheek. "You play the ingenue well, Lady Graham," he said, sitting upright to better meet her frankly sensual gaze. His pale blue eyes had warmed, restoring a goodly measure of his charm. "I'd be a damned fool to mind," he said, his grin in sharp contrast to the curious affection in his eyes.

Exhaling theatrically, Elizabeth said, "Thank you, my lord," in a blatant parody of gratitude. "Without your assistance I despaired of properly arousing you."

He laughed, a warm-hearted sound of natural pleasure. "On that count you needn't have worried. I've been in rut since I left Edinburgh to see you."

"Could I be of some help?" she murmured, her voice husky, enticing.

He found himself attentively searching the ground for a suitable place to lie with her. "I warn you," he said very low, his mouth in a lazy grin, "I'm days past the need for seduction. All I can offer you is this country setting. Do you mind?"

She smiled up at him as she put her hand in his. "As long as you hold me, my lord, and as long as the grass stains don't show."

He paused for a moment with her small hand light on his palm. "You're very remarkable," he softly said.

"Too candid for you, my lord?" she playfully inquired.

His long fingers closed around her hand in an act of possession, pure and simple, as if he would keep this spirited, plain-speaking woman who startled him. "Your candor excites me," he said. "Be warned," he murmured, drawing her to her feet. "I've been wanting you for three days' past; I won't guarantee finesse." Releasing her hand, he held his up so she could see them tremble. "Look."

"I'm shaking *inside* so violently I may savage you first, my lord," Elizabeth softly breathed, swaying toward him, her fragrance sweet in his nostrils, her face lifted for a kiss. "I've been waiting four months since I left Goldiehouse."

A spiking surge of lust ripped through his senses, gut-deep, searing, her celibacy a singular, flamboyant ornament offered to him as if it were his duty, his obligation to bring her pleasure. In a flashing moment his hands closed on her shoulders. Pulling her sharply close, his palms slid down her back—then lower, swiftly cupping her bottom. His mouth dipped to hers and he forced her mouth open, plunging his tongue deep inside.

Like a woman too long denied, Elizabeth welcomed him, pulling his head down so she could reach his mouth more easily, straining upward on tiptoes so she could feel him hard against her, tearing at the buttons on his shirt so the heat of his skin touched hers.

"Hurry, Johnnie, please . . ." she whispered.

Moonlight, Madness, & Magic

by

Suzanne Foster, Charlotte Hughes, and Olivia Rupprecht

"A beguiling mix of passion and the occult. . . . an engaging read."
—*Publishers Weekly*
"Incredibly ingenious." —*Romantic Times*

This strikingly original anthology by three of Loveswept's bestselling authors is one of the most talked about books of the year! With more than 2.5 million copies of their titles in print, these beloved authors bring their talents to a boldly imaginative collection of romantic novellas that weaves a tale of witchcraft, passion, and unconditional love set in 1785, 1872, and 1992.

Here's a look at the heart-stopping prologue . . . .

OXFORD VILLAGE, MASSACHUSETTS — 1690 Rachael Deliverance Dobbs had been beautiful once. The flaming red hair that often strayed from her morning cap and curled in wispy tendrils about her face had turned more than one shop-keeper's head. Today, however, that red hair was tangled and filthy and fell against her back and shoulders like a tattered woolen shawl.

Prison had not served her well.

"The woman hath *witchcraft* in her," an onlooker spat out as Rachael was led to the front of the meeting house, where a constable, the governor's magistrate, and several of the town selectmen waited to decide her fate. Her ankles were shackled in irons, making her progress slow and painful.

Rachael staggered, struggling to catch her balance as the magistrate peered over his spectacles at her. Clearing his throat, the magistrate began to speak, giving each word a deep and thunderous import. "Rachael Deliverance Dobbs, thou hast been accused by this court of not fearing the Almighty God as do thy good and prudent neighbors, of preternatural acts against the citizenry of Oxford, and of the heinous crime of witchcraft, for which, by the law of the colony of Massachusetts, thou deservest to die. Has thou anything to say in thy defense?"

Rachael Dobbs could barely summon the strength to deny the charges. Her accusers had kept her jailed for months, often depriving her of sleep, food, and clean water to drink. In order to secure a confession, they'd whipped her with rawhide and tortured her with hideous instruments. Though she'd been grievously injured and several of her ribs broken, she'd given them nothing.

"Nay," she said faintly, "I know not of which ye speak, m'lord. For as God is my witness, I have been wrongly accused."

A rage quickened the air, and several of the spectators rose from their seats. "Blasphemy!" someone cried. "The witch would use *His* name in vain?"

"Order!" The magistrate brought his gavel down. "Let the accused answer the charges. Goody Dobbs, it is said thou makest the devil's brew of strange plants that grow in the forest."

"I know not this devil's brew you speak of," Rachael protested. "I use the herbs for healing, just as my mother before me."

"And thou extracts a fungus from rye grass to stop birthing pains?" he queried.

"I do not believe a woman should suffer so, m'lord."

"Even though the Good Book commands it?"

"The Good Book also commands us to use the sense God gave us," she reminded him tremulously.

"I'll not tolerate this sacrilege!" The village preacher slammed his fist down on the table, inciting the onlookers into a frenzy of shouting and name-calling.

As the magistrate called for order, Rachael turned to the crowd, searching for the darkly handsome face of her betrothed, Jonathan Nightingale. She'd not been allowed visitors in jail, but surely Jonathan would be here today to speak on her behalf. With his wealth and good name, he would quickly put an end to this hysteria. That hope had kept her alive, bringing her comfort even when she'd learned her children had been placed in the care of Jonathan's housekeeper, a young woman Rachael distrusted for her deceptive ways. But that mattered little now. When Jonathaan cleared her name of these crimes, she would be united with her babes once again. How she longed to see them!

"Speak thou for me, Jonathan Nightingale?" she cried, forgetting everything but her joy at seeing him. "Thou knowest me better than anyone. Thou knowest the secrets of my heart. Tell these people I am not what they accuse me. Tell them, so that my children may be returned to me." Her voice trembled with emotion, but as Jonathan glanced up and met her eyes, she knew a moment of doubt. She didn't see the welcoming warmth she expected. Was something amiss?

At the magistrate's instruction, the bailiff called Jonathan to come forward. "State thy name for the court," the bailiff said, once he'd been sworn in.

"Jonathan Peyton Nightingale."

"Thou knowest the accused, Goody Dobbs?" the magistrate asked.

Jonathan acknowledged Rachael with a slow nod of his head. "Mistress Dobbs and I were engaged to be married before she was incarcerated," Jonathan told the magistrate. "I've assumed the care of her children these last few months. She has no family of her own."

"Hast thou anything to say in her defense?"

"She was a decent mother, to be sure. Her children be well mannered."

"And have ye reason to believe the charges against her?"

When Jonathan hesitated, the magistrate pressed him. "Prithee, do not withhold information from the court, Mr. Nightingale," he cautioned, "lest thee find thyself in the same dire predicament as the accused. Conspiring to protect a witch is a lawful test of guilt."

Startled, Jonathan could only stare at the stern-faced tribunal before him. It had never occured to him that his association with Rachael could put him in a hangman's noose as well. He had been searching his soul since she'd been jailed, wondering how much he was morally bound to reveal at this trial. Now he saw little choice but to unburden himself.

"After she was taken, I found this among her things," he said, pulling an object from his coat pocket and unwrapping it. He avoided looking at Rachael, anticipating the stricken expression he would surely see in her eyes. "It's an image made of horsehair. A woman's image. There be a pin stuck through it."

The crowd gasped as Jonathan held up the effigy. A woman screamed, and even the magistrate drew back in horror.

Rachael sat in stunned disbelief. An icy fist closed around her heart. How could Jonathan have done such a thing? Did he not realize he'd signed her death warrant? Dear merciful God, if they found her guilty, she would never see her children again!

" 'Twas mere folly that I fashioned the image, m'lord," she told the magistrate. "I suspected my betrothed of dallying with his housekeeper. I fear my temper bested me."

"And was it folly when thou gavest Goodwife Brown's child the evil eye and caused her to languish with the fever?" the magistrate probed.

" 'Twas coincidence, m'lord," she said, imploring him to believe her. "The child was ill when I arrived at Goody Brown's house. I merely tried to help her." Rachael could see the magistrate's skepticism, and she whirled to Jonathan in desperation. "How canst thou doubt me, Jonathan?" she asked.

He hung his head. He was torn with regret, even shame. He loved Rachael, but God help him, he had no wish to die beside her. One had only to utter the word *witch* these days to end up on the gallows. Not that Rachael hadn't given all of them cause to suspect her. When he'd found the effigy, he'd told himself she must have been maddened by jealousy. But truly he didn't understand her anymore. She'd stopped going to Sunday services and more than once had induced him to lie abed with her on a Sabbath morn. "Methinks thou hast bewitched me as well, Rachael," he replied.

Another gasp from the crowd.

"Hanging is too good for her!" a woman shouted.

"Burn her!" another cried from the front row. "Before she bewitches us all."

Rachael bent her head in despair, all hope draining from her. Her own betrothed had forsaken her, and his condemnation meant certain death. There was no one who could save her now. And yet, in the depths of her desolation, a spark of rage kindled.

"So be it," she said, seized by a black hysteria. She was beyond caring now, beyond the crowd's censure or their grace. No one could take anything more from her than had already been taken. Jonathan's engagement gift to her, a golden locket, hung at her neck. She ripped it free and flung it at him.

"Thou shall have thy desire, Jonathan Nightingale," she cried. "And pay for it dearly. Since thou hast consigned me to the gallows and stolen my children from me, I shall put a blood curse on thee and thine."

The magistrate pounded his gavel against the table, ordering the spectators to silence. "Mistress Dobbs!" he warned, his voice harsh, "I fear thou hast just sealed thy fate."

But Rachael would not be deterred. Her heart was aflame with the fury of a woman betrayed. "Hear me good, Jonathan," she said, oblivious of the magistrate, of everyone but the man she'd once loved with all her being. "Thou hast damned my soul to hell, but I'll not burn there alone. I curse the Nightingale seed to a fate worse than the flames of Hades. Your progeny shall be as the living dead, denied the rest of the grave."

Her voice dropped to a terrifying hush as she began to intone the curse. "The third son of every third son shall walk the earth as a creature of the night, trapped in shadows, no two creatures alike. Stripped of humanity, he will howl in concert with demons, never to die, always to wander in agony, until a woman entraps his heart and soul as thee did mine—"

"My God, she is truly the devil's mistress!" the preacher gasped. A cry rose from the crowd, and several of them surged forward, trying to stop her. Guards rushed to block them.

"Listen to me, Jonathan!" Rachael cried over the din. "I've not finished with thee yet. If that woman should find a way to set the creature free, it will be at great and terrible cost. A sacrifice no mortal woman would ever be willing to make—"

She hesitated, her chin beginning to tremble as hot tears pooled in her eyes. Glistening, they slid down her cheeks, burning her tender flesh before they dropped to the wooden floor. But as they hit the planks, something astonishing happened. Even

Rachael in her grief was amazed. The teardrops hardened before everyone's eyes into precious gems. Flashing in the sunlight was a dazzling blue-white diamond, a blood-red ruby, and a brilliant green emerald.

The crowd was stunned to silence.

Rachael glanced up, aware of Jonathan's fear, of everyone's astonishment. Their gaping stares brought her a fleeting sense of triumph. Her curse had been heard.

"Rachael Dobbs, confess thy sins before this court and thy Creator!" the magistrate bellowed.

But it was too late for confessions. The doors to the courtroom burst open, and a pack of men streamed in with blazing pine torches. "Goody Brown's child is dead of the fits," they shouted. "The witch must burn!"

The guards couldn't hold back the vigilantes, and Rachael closed her eyes as the pack of men engulfed her. She said a silent good-bye to her children as she was gripped by bruising hands and lifted off the ground. She could feel herself being torn nearly apart as they dragged her from the meeting room, but she did not cry out. She felt no physical pain. She had just made a pact with the forces of darkness, and she could no longer feel anything except the white-hot inferno of the funeral pyre that would soon release her to her everlasting vigil.

She welcomed it, just as she welcomed the sweet justice that would one day be hers. She would not die in vain. Her curse had been heard.

Satin and Steele
by
Fayrene Preston

SATIN AND STEELE *is a classic favorite of fans of
Fayrene Preston. Originally published under the pseud-
onym Jaelyn Conlee, this novel was the talented Ms.
Preston's first ever published novel. We are thrilled to
offer you the opportunity to read this long-unavailable
book in its new Bantam edition.*

Skye Anderson knew the joy and wonder of love—as
well as the pain of its tragic loss. She'd carved a new
life for herself at Dallas' Hayes Corporation, finding
security in a cocoon of hard-working days and lonely
nights. Then her company is taken over by the leg-
endary corporate raider James Steele and once again
Skye must face the possibility of losing everything
she cares about. When Steele enlists her aid in
organizing the new company, she is determined to
prove herself worthy of the challenge. But as they
work together side by side, Skye can't deny that
she feels more than a professional interest in her

new boss—and that the feeling is mutual. Soon she would have to decide whether to let go of her desire for Steele once and for all—or risk everything for a second chance at love.

And don't miss these heart-stopping romances from Bantam Books, on sale in November:

ADAM'S FALL
a new hardcover edition of the Sandra Brown classic!

NOTORIOUS
by Patricia Potter
The *Romantic Times* 1992
"Storyteller of the Year"

PRINCESS OF THIEVES
by Katherine O'Neal
"A brilliant new talent bound to make her mark on the genre." —Iris Johansen

CAPTURE THE NIGHT
by Geralyn Dawson
"A fresh and delightful new author!
GOLD 5 stars"
—*Heartland Critiques*

and in hardcover from Doubleday

ON WINGS OF MAGIC
a classic romance by Kay Hooper

OFFICIAL RULES

To enter the sweepstakes below carefully follow all instructions found elsewhere in this offer.

The **Winners Classic** will award prizes with the following approximate maximum values: 1 Grand Prize: $26,500 (or $25,000 cash alternate); 1 First Prize: $3,000; 5 Second Prizes: $400 each; 35 Third Prizes: $100 each; 1,000 Fourth Prizes: $7.50 each. Total maximum retail value of Winners Classic Sweepstakes is $42,500. Some presentations of this sweepstakes may contain individual entry numbers corresponding to one or more of the aforementioned prize levels. To determine the Winners, individual entry numbers will first be compared with the winning numbers preselected by computer. For winning numbers not returned, prizes will be awarded in random drawings from among all eligible entries received. Prize choices may be offered at various levels. If a winner chooses an automobile prize, all license and registration fees, taxes, destination charges and, other expenses not offered herein are the responsibility of the winner. If a winner chooses a trip, travel must be complete within one year from the time the prize is awarded. Minors must be accompanied by an adult. Travel companion(s) must also sign release of liability. Trips are subject to space and departure availability. Certain black-out dates may apply.

The following applies to the sweepstakes named above:

No purchase necessary. You can also enter the sweepstakes by sending your name and address to: P.O. Box 508, Gibbstown, N.J. 08027. Mail each entry separately. Sweepstakes begins 6/1/93. Entries must be received by 12/30/94. Not responsible for lost, late, damaged, misdirected, illegible or postage due mail. Mechanically reproduced entries are not eligible. All entries become property of the sponsor and will not be returned.

Prize Selection/Validations: Selection of winners will be conducted no later than 5:00 PM on January 28, 1995, by an independent judging organization whose decisions are final. Random drawings will be held at 1211 Avenue of the Americas, New York, N.Y. 10036. Entrants need not be present to win. Odds of winning are determined by total number of entries received. Circulation of this sweepstakes is estimated not to exceed 200 million. All prizes are guaranteed to be awarded and delivered to winners. Winners will be notified by mail and may be required to complete an affidavit of eligibility and release of liability which must be returned within 14 days of date on notification and alternate winners will be selected in a random drawing. Any prize notification letter or any prize returned to a participating sponsor, Bantam Doubleday Dell Publishing Group, Inc., its participating divisions or subsidiaries, or the independent judging organization as undeliverable will be awarded to an alternate winner. Prizes are not transferable. No substitution for prizes except as offered or as may be necessary due to unavailability, in which case a prize of equal or greater value will be awarded. Prizes will be awarded approximately 90 days after the drawing. All taxes are the sole responsibility of the winners. Entry constitutes permission (except where prohibited by law) to use winners' names, hometowns, and likenesses for publicity purposes without further or other compensation. Prizes won by minors will be awarded in the name of parent or legal guardian.

Participation: Sweepstakes open to residents of the United States and Canada, except for the province of Quebec. Sweepstakes sponsored by Bantam Doubleday Dell Publishing Group, Inc., (BDD), 1540 Broadway, New York, NY 10036. Versions of this sweepstakes with different graphics and prize choices will be offered in conjunction with various solicitations or promotions by different subsidiaries and divisions of BDD. Where applicable, winners will have their choice of any prize offered at level won. Employees of BDD, its divisions, subsidiaries, advertising agencies, independent judging organization, and their immediate family members are not eligible.

Canadian residents, in order to win, must first correctly answer a time limited arithmetical skill testing question. Void in Puerto Rico, Quebec and wherever prohibited or restricted by law. Subject to all federal, state, local and provincial laws and regulations. For a list of major prize winners (available after 1/29/95): send a self-addressed, stamped envelope entirely separate from your entry to: Sweepstakes Winners, P.O. Box 517, Gibbstown, NJ 08027. Requests must be received by 12/30/94. DO NOT SEND ANY OTHER CORRESPONDENCE TO THIS P.O. BOX.

Don't miss these fabulous Bantam women's fiction titles

on sale in November

• NOTORIOUS

by Patricia Potter, author of *RENEGADE*

Long ago, Catalina Hilliard had vowed never to give away her heart, but she hadn't counted on the spark of desire that flared between her and her business rival, Marsh Canton. Now that desire is about to spin Cat's carefully orchestrated life out of control.

_____56225-8 $5.50/6.50 in Canada

• PRINCESS OF THIEVES

by Katherine O'Neal, author of *THE LAST HIGHWAYMAN*

Mace Blackwood was a daring rogue—the greatest con artist in the world. Saranda Sherwin was a master thief who used her wits and wiles to make tough men weak. And when Saranda's latest charade leads to tragedy and sends her fleeing for her life, Mace is compelled to follow, no matter what the cost.

_____56066-2 $5.50/$6.50 in Canada

• CAPTURE THE NIGHT

by Geralyn Dawson

In this "Once Upon a Time" Romance with "Beauty and the Beast" at its heart, Geralyn Dawson weaves the love story of a runaway beauty, the Texan who rescues her, and their precious stolen "Rose."

_____56176-6 $4.99/5.99 in Canada

Ask for these books at your local bookstore or use this page to order.

❏ Please send me the books I have checked above. I am enclosing $ _____ (add $2.50 to cover postage and handling). Send check or money order, no cash or C. O. D.'s please.

Name _____

Address _____

City/ State/ Zip _____

Send order to: Bantam Books, Dept. FN121, 2451 S. Wolf Rd., Des Plaines, IL 60018

Allow four to six weeks for delivery.

Prices and availability subject to change without notice.

FN121 11/9█